Betty Neels sadly passed away in 2001. As one of our best-loved authors, Betty will be greatly missed, both by her friends at Mills & Boon and by her legions of loyal readers around the world. Betty was a prolific writer and has left a lasting legacy through her heartwarming novels, and she will always be remembered as a truly delightful person who brought great happiness to many.

This special collection of Betty's best-loved books, are all available in Large Print, making them an easier read on your eyes, and ensuring you won't miss any of the romance in Betty's ever-popular novels.

The Betty Neels Large Print Collection

ALWAYS
AND FOREVER

BY

BETTY NEELS

MILLS & BOON®

Pure reading pleasure™

First Published in Great Britain 1999
Large Print Edition 2008
Harlequin Mills & Boon Limited,
Eton House, 18-24 Paradise Road,
Richmond, Surrey TW9 1SR

© Betty Neels 1999

ISBN: 978 0 263 20463 6

Set in Times Roman 16½ on 20¾ pt.
32-0708-53321

Printed and bound in Great Britain
by Antony Rowe Ltd, Chippenham, Wiltshire

CHAPTER ONE

THERE was going to be a storm; the blue sky of a summer evening was slowly being swallowed by black clouds, heavy with rain and thunder, flashing warning signals of flickering lightning over the peaceful Dorset countryside, casting gloom over the village. The girl gathering a line of washing from the small orchard behind the house standing on the village outskirts paused to study the sky before lugging the washing basket through the open door at the back of the house.

She was a small girl, nicely plump, with a face which, while not pretty, was redeemed by fine brown eyes. Her pale brown hair was gathered in an untidy bunch on the top of her head and she was wearing a cotton dress which had seen better days.

She put the basket down, closed the door and

went in search of candles and matches, then put two old-fashioned oil lamps on the wooden table. If the storm was bad there would be a power cut before the evening was far advanced.

This done to her satisfaction, she poked up the elderly Aga, set a kettle to boil and turned her attention to the elderly dog and battle-scarred old tomcat, waiting patiently for their suppers.

She got their food, talking while she did so because the eerie quiet before the storm broke was a little unnerving, and then made tea and sat down to drink it as the first heavy drops of rain began to fall.

With the rain came a sudden wind which sent her round the house shutting windows against the deluge. Back in the kitchen, she addressed the dog.

'Well, there won't be anyone coming now,' she told him, and gave a small shriek as lightning flashed and thunder drowned out any other sound. She sat down at the table and he came and sat beside her, and, after a moment, the cat got onto her lap.

The wind died down as suddenly as it had

arisen but the storm was almost overhead. It had become very dark and the almost continuous flashes made it seem even darker. Presently the light over the table began to flicker; she prudently lit a candle before it went out.

She got up then, lighted the lamps and took one into the hall before sitting down again. There was nothing to do but to wait until the storm had passed.

The lull was shattered by a peal on the doorbell, so unexpected that she sat for a moment, not quite believing it. But a second prolonged peal sent her to the door, lamp in hand.

A man stood in the porch. She held the lamp high in order to get a good look at him; he was a very large man, towering over her.

'I saw your sign. Can you put us up for the night? I don't care to drive further in this weather.'

He had a quiet voice and he looked genuine. 'Who's we?' she asked.

'My mother and myself.'

She slipped the chain off the door. 'Come in.' She peered round him. 'Is that your car?'

'Yes—is there a garage?'

'Go round the side of the house; there's a barn—the door's open. There's plenty of room there.'

He nodded and turned back to the car to open its door and help his mother out. Ushering them into the hall, the girl said, 'Come back in through the kitchen door; I'll leave it unlocked. It's across the yard from the barn.'

He nodded again, a man of few words, she supposed, and he went outside. She turned to look at her second guest. The woman was tall, good-looking, in her late fifties, she supposed, and dressed with understated elegance.

'Would you like to see your room? And would you like a meal? It's a bit late to cook dinner but you could have an omelette or scrambled eggs and bacon with tea or coffee?'

The older woman put out a hand. 'Mrs Fforde—spelt with two ffs, I'm afraid. My son's a doctor; he was driving me to the other side of Glastonbury, taking a shortcut, but driving had become impossible. Your sign was like something from heaven.' She had to raise her voice against the heavenly din.

The girl offered a hand. 'Amabel Parsons. I'm sorry you had such a horrid journey.'

'I hate storms, don't you? You're not alone in the house?'

'Well, yes, I am, but I have Cyril—that's my dog—and Oscar the cat.' Amabel hesitated. 'Would you like to come into the sitting room until Dr Fforde comes? Then you can decide if you would like something to eat. I'm afraid you will have to go to bed by candlelight…'

She led the way down the hall and into a small room, comfortably furnished with easy chairs and a small round table. There were shelves of books on either side of the fireplace and a large window across which Amabel drew the curtains before setting the lamp on the table.

'I'll unlock the kitchen door,' she said and hurried back to the kitchen just in time to admit the doctor.

He was carrying two cases. 'Shall I take these up?'

'Yes, please. I'll ask Mrs Fforde if she would like to go to her room now. I asked if you would like anything to eat…'

'Most emphatically yes. That's if it's not putting you to too much trouble. Anything will do—sandwiches…'

'Omelettes, scrambled eggs, bacon and eggs? I did explain to Mrs Fforde that it's too late to cook a full meal.'

He smiled down at her. 'I'm sure Mother is longing for a cup of tea, and omelettes sound fine.' He glanced round him. 'You're not alone?'

'Yes,' said Amabel. 'I'll take you upstairs.'

She gave them the two rooms at the front of the house and pointed out the bathroom. 'Plenty of hot water,' she added, before going back to the kitchen.

When they came downstairs presently she had the table laid in the small room and offered them omelettes, cooked to perfection, toast and butter and a large pot of tea. This had kept her busy, but it had also kept her mind off the storm, still raging above their heads. It rumbled away finally in the small hours, but by the time she had cleared up the supper things and prepared the breakfast table, she was too tired to notice.

She was up early, but so was Dr Fforde. He

accepted the tea she offered him before he wandered out of the door into the yard and the orchard beyond, accompanied by Cyril. He presently strolled back to stand in the doorway and watch her getting their breakfast.

Amabel, conscious of his steady gaze, said briskly, 'Would Mrs Fforde like breakfast in bed? It's no extra trouble.'

'I believe she would like that very much. I'll have mine with you here.'

'Oh, you can't do that.' She was taken aback. 'I mean, your breakfast is laid in the sitting room. I'll bring it to you whenever you're ready.'

'I dislike eating alone. If you put everything for Mother on a tray I'll carry it up.'

He was friendly in a casual way, but she guessed that he was a man who disliked arguing. She got a tray ready, and when he came downstairs again and sat down at the kitchen table she put a plate of bacon, eggs and mushrooms in front of him, adding toast and marmalade before pouring the tea.

'Come and sit down and eat your breakfast and tell me why you live here alone,' he invited. He sounded so like an elder brother or a kind uncle that she did so, watching him demolish his breakfast with evident enjoyment before loading a slice of toast with butter and marmalade.

She had poured herself a cup of tea, but whatever he said she wasn't going to eat her breakfast with him…

He passed her the slice of toast. 'Eat that up and tell me why you live alone.'

'Well, really!' began Amabel and then, meeting his kindly look, added, 'It's only for a month or so. My mother's gone to Canada,' she told him. 'My married sister lives there and she's just had a baby. It was such a good opportunity for her to go. You see, in the summer we get quite a lot of people coming just for bed and breakfast, like you, so I'm not really alone. It's different in the winter, of course.'

He asked, 'You don't mind being here by yourself? What of the days—and nights—when no one wants bed and breakfast?'

She said defiantly, 'I have Cyril, and Oscar's splendid company. Besides, there's the phone.'

'And your nearest neighbour?' he asked idly.

'Old Mrs Drew, round the bend in the lane going to the village. Also, it's only half a mile to the village.' She still sounded defiant.

He passed his cup for more tea. Despite her brave words he suspected that she wasn't as self-assured as she would have him believe. A plain girl, he considered, but nice eyes, nice voice and apparently not much interest in clothes; the denim skirt and cotton blouse were crisp and spotless, but could hardly be called fashionable. He glanced at her hands, which were small and well shaped, bearing signs of housework.

He said, 'A lovely morning after the storm. That's a pleasant orchard you have beyond the yard. And a splendid view...'

'Yes, it's splendid all the year round.'

'Do you get cut off in the winter?'

'Yes, sometimes. Would you like more tea?'

'No, thank you. I'll see if my mother is getting ready to leave.' He smiled at her. 'That was a delicious meal.' But not, he reflected, a very friendly one. Amabel Parsons had given him the strong impression that she wished him out of the house.

Within the hour he and his mother had gone, driving away in the dark blue Rolls Royce. Amabel stood in the open doorway, watching it disappear round the bend in the lane. It had been providential, she told herself, that they should have stopped at the house at the height of the storm; they had kept her busy and she hadn't had the time to be frightened. They had been no trouble—and she needed the money.

It would be nice, she thought wistfully, to have someone like Dr Fforde as a friend. Sitting at breakfast with him, she'd had an urgent desire to talk to him, tell him how lonely she was, and sometimes a bit scared, how tired she was of making up beds and getting breakfast for a suc-cession of strangers, keeping the place going until her mother returned, and all the while keeping up the façade of an independent and competent young woman perfectly able to manage on her own.

That was necessary, otherwise well-meaning

people in the village would have made it their business to dissuade her mother from her trip and even suggest that Amabel should shut up the house and go and stay with a great-aunt she hardly knew, who lived in Yorkshire and who certainly wouldn't want her.

Amabel went back into the house, collected up the bedlinen and made up the beds again; hopefully there would be more guests later in the day…

She readied the rooms, inspected the contents of the fridge and the deep freeze, hung out the washing and made herself a sandwich before going into the orchard with Cyril and Oscar. They sat, the three of them, on an old wooden bench, nicely secluded from the lane but near enough to hear if anyone called.

Which they did, just as she was on the point of going indoors for her tea.

The man on the doorstep turned round impatiently as she reached him.

'I rang twice. I want bed and breakfast for my wife, son and daughter.'

Amabel turned to look at the car. There was a

young man in the driver's seat, and a middle-
aged woman and a girl sitting in the back.

'Three rooms? Certainly. But I must tell you
that there is only one bathroom, although there
are handbasins in the rooms.'

He said rudely, 'I suppose that's all we can
expect in this part of the world. We took a wrong
turning and landed ourselves here, at the back of
beyond. What do you charge? And we do get a
decent breakfast?'

Amabel told him, 'Yes.' As her mother frequently
reminded her, it took all sorts to make the world.

The three people in the car got out: a bossy
woman, the girl pretty but sulky, and the young
man looking at her in a way she didn't like...

They inspected their rooms with loud-voiced
comments about old-fashioned furniture and no
more than one bathroom—and that laughably
old-fashioned. And they wanted tea: sandwiches
and scones and cake. 'And plenty of jam,' the
young man shouted after her as she left the room.

After tea they wanted to know where the
TV was.

'I haven't got a television.'

They didn't believe her. 'Everyone has a TV set,' complained the girl. 'Whatever are we going to do this evening?'

'The village is half a mile down the lane,' said Amabel. 'There's a pub there, and you can get a meal, if you wish.'

'Better than hanging around here.'

It was a relief to see them climb back into the car and drive off presently. She laid the table for their breakfast and put everything ready in the kitchen before getting herself some supper. It was a fine light evening, so she strolled into the orchard and sat down on the bench. Dr Fforde and his mother would be at Glastonbury, she supposed, staying with family or friends. He would be married, of course, to a pretty girl with lovely clothes—there would be a small boy and a smaller girl, and they would live in a large and comfortable house; he was successful, for he drove a Rolls Royce…

Conscious that she was feeling sad, as well as wasting her time, she went back indoors and made out the bill; there might not be time in the morning.

She was up early the next morning; breakfast was to be ready by eight o'clock, she had been told on the previous evening—a decision she'd welcomed with relief. Breakfast was eaten, the bill paid—but only after double-checking everything on it and some scathing comments about the lack of modern amenities.

Amabel waited politely at the door until they had driven away then went to put the money in the old tea caddy on the kitchen dresser. It added substantially to the contents but it had been hard earned!

The rooms, as she'd expected, had been left in a disgraceful state. She flung open the window, stripped beds and set about turning them back to their usual pristine appearance. It was still early, and it was a splendid morning, so she filled the washing machine and started on the breakfast dishes.

By midday everything was just as it should be. She made sandwiches and took them and a mug of coffee out to the orchard with Cyril and Oscar for company, and sat down to read the letter from her mother the postman had brought. Everything was splendid, she wrote. The baby was thriving and she had decided to stay another few weeks, if Amabel could manage for a little longer—*For I don't suppose I'll be able to visit here for a year or two, unless something turns up.*

Which was true enough, and it made sense too. Her mother had taken out a loan so that she could go to Canada, and even though it was a small one it would have to be paid off before she went again.

Amabel put the letter in her pocket, divided the rest of her sandwich between Cyril and Oscar and went back into the house. There was always the chance that someone would come around teatime and ask for a meal, so she would make a cake and a batch of scones.

It was as well that she did; she had just taken them out of the Aga when the doorbell rang and two elderly ladies enquired if she would give them bed and breakfast.

They had come in an old Morris, and, while well-spoken and tidily dressed, she judged them to be not too free with their money. But they looked nice and she had a kind heart.

'If you would share a twin-bedded room?' she suggested. 'The charge is the same for two people as one.' She told them how much and added, 'Two breakfasts, of course, and if you would like tea?'

They glanced at each other. 'Thank you. Would you serve us a light supper later?'

'Certainly. If you would fetch your cases? The car can go into the barn at the side of the house.'

Amabel gave them a good tea, and while they went for a short walk, she got supper—salmon fish cakes, of tinned salmon, of course, potatoes whipped to a satiny smoothness, and peas from the garden. She popped an egg custard into the oven by way of afters and was rewarded by their genteel thanks.

She ate her own supper in the kitchen, took them a pot of tea and wished them goodnight. In the morning she gave them boiled eggs, toast and marmalade and a pot of coffee, and all with a generous hand.

She hadn't made much money, but it had been nice to see their elderly faces light up. And they had left her a tip, discreetly put on one of the bedside tables. As for the bedroom, they had left it so neat it was hard to see that anyone had been in it.

She added the money to the tea caddy and decided that tomorrow she would go to the village and pay it into the post office account, stock up on groceries and get meat from the butcher's van which called twice a week at the village.

It was a lovely morning again, and her spirits rose despite her disappointment at her mother's delayed return home. She wasn't doing too badly with bed and breakfast, and she was adding steadily to their savings. There were the winter months to think of, of course, but she might be able to get a part-time job once her mother was home.

She went into the garden to pick peas, singing cheerfully and slightly off key.

Nobody came that day, and the following day only a solitary woman on a walking holiday came in the early evening; she went straight to bed after a pot of tea and left the next morning after an early breakfast.

After she had gone, Amabel discovered that she had taken the towels with her.

Two disappointing days, reflected Amabel. I wonder what will happen tomorrow?

She was up early again, for there was no point in lying in bed when it was daylight soon after five o'clock. She breakfasted, tidied the house, did a pile of ironing before the day got too hot, and then wandered out to the bench in the orchard. It was far too early for any likely person to want a room, and she would hear if a car stopped in the lane.

But of course one didn't hear a Rolls Royce, for it made almost no sound.

Dr Fforde got out and stood looking at the house. It was a pleasant place, somewhat in need of small repairs and a lick of paint, but its small windows shone and the brass knocker on its solid front door was burnished to a dazzling brightness. He trod round the side of the house, past the barn, and saw Amabel sitting between Cyril and Oscar. Since she was a girl who couldn't abide being idle, she was shelling peas.

He stood watching her for a moment, wondering why he had wanted to see her again. True, she had interested him, so small, plain and pot valiant, and so obviously terrified of the storm—and very much at the mercy of undesirable characters who might choose to call. Surely she had an aunt or cousin who could come and stay with her?

It was none of his business, of course, but it had seemed a good idea to call and see her since he was on his way to Glastonbury.

He stepped onto the rough gravel of the yard so that she looked up.

She got to her feet, and her smile left him in no doubt that she was glad to see him.

He said easily, 'Good morning. I'm on my way to Glastonbury. Have you quite recovered from the storm?'

'Oh, yes.' She added honestly, 'But I was frightened, you know. I was so very glad when you and your mother came.'

She collected up the colander of peas and came towards him. 'Would you like a cup of coffee?'

'Yes, please.' He followed her into the kitchen

and sat down at the table and thought how restful she was; she had seemed glad to see him, but she had probably learned to give a welcoming smile to anyone who knocked on the door. Certainly she had displayed no fuss at seeing him.

He said on an impulse, 'Will you have lunch with me? There's a pub—the Old Boot in Underthorn—fifteen minutes' drive from here. I don't suppose you get any callers before the middle of the afternoon?'

She poured the coffee and fetched a tin of biscuits.

'But you're on your way to Glastonbury…'

'Yes, but not expected until teatime. And it's such a splendid day.' When she hesitated he said, 'We could take Cyril with us.'

She said then, 'Thank you; I should like that. But I must be back soon after two o'clock; it's Saturday…'

They went back to the orchard presently, and sat on the bench while Amabel finished shelling the peas. Oscar had got onto the doctor's knee and Cyril had sprawled under his feet. They talked idly about nothing much and Amabel, quite at her ease, now answered his carefully put questions without realising just how much she was telling him until she stopped in mid-sentence, aware that her tongue was running away with her. He saw that at once and began to talk about something else.

They drove to the Old Boot Inn just before noon and found a table on the rough grass at its back. There was a small river, overshadowed by trees, and since it was early there was no one else there. They ate home-made pork pies with salad, and drank iced lemonade which the landlord's wife made herself. Cyril sat at their feet with a bowl of water and a biscuit.

The landlord, looking at them from the bar window, observed to his wife, 'Look happy, don't they?'

And they were, all three of them, although the doctor hadn't identified his feeling as happiness, merely pleasant content at the glorious morning and the undemanding company.

He drove Amabel back presently and, rather to

her surprise, parked the car in the yard behind the house, got out, took the door key from her and unlocked the back door.

Oscar came to meet them and he stooped to stroke him. 'May I sit in the orchard for a little while?' he asked. 'I seldom get the chance to sit quietly in such peaceful surroundings.'

Amabel stopped herself just in time from saying, 'You poor man,' and said instead, 'Of course you may, for as long as you like. Would you like a cup of tea, or an apple?'

So he sat on the bench chewing an apple, with Oscar on his knee, aware that his reason for sitting there was to cast an eye over any likely guests in the hope that before he went a respectable middle-aged pair would have decided to stay.

He was to have his wish. Before very long a middle-aged pair did turn up, with mother-in-law, wishing to stay for two nights. It was absurd, he told himself, that he should feel concern. Amabel was a perfectly capable young woman, and able to look after herself; besides, she had a telephone.

He went to the open kitchen door and found her there, getting tea.

'I must be off,' he told her. 'Don't stop what you're doing. I enjoyed my morning.'

She was cutting a large cake into neat slices. 'So did I. Thank you for my lunch.' She smiled at him. 'Go carefully, Dr Fforde.'

She carried the tea tray into the drawing room and went back to the kitchen. They were three nice people—polite, and anxious not to be too much trouble. 'An evening meal?' they had asked diffidently, and had accepted her offer of jacket potatoes and salad, fruit tart and coffee with pleased smiles. They would go for a short walk presently, the man told her, and when would she like to serve their supper?

When they had gone she made the tart, put the potatoes in the oven and went to the vegetable patch by the orchard to get a lettuce and radishes. There was no hurry, so she sat down on the bench and thought about the day.

She had been surprised to see the doctor again. She had been pleased too. She had thought about him, but she hadn't expected to see him again; when she had looked up and seen him standing there it had been like seeing an old friend.

'Nonsense,' said Amabel loudly. 'He came this morning because he wanted a cup of coffee.' What about taking you out to lunch? asked a persistent voice at the back of her mind.

'He's probably a man who doesn't like to eat alone.'

And, having settled the matter, she went back to the kitchen.

The three guests intended to spend Sunday touring around the countryside. They would return at tea time and could they have supper? They added that they would want to leave early the next morning, which left Amabel with almost all day free to do as she wanted.

There was no need for her to stay at the house; she didn't intend to let the third room if anyone called. She would go to church and then spend a quiet afternoon with the Sunday paper.

She liked going to church, for she met friends and acquaintances and could have a chat, and at the same time assure anyone who asked that her mother would be coming home soon and that she herself was perfectly content on her own. She was aware that some of the older members of the congregation didn't approve of her mother's trip and thought that at the very least some friend or cousin should have moved in with Amabel.

It was something she and her mother had discussed at some length, until her mother had burst into tears, declaring that she wouldn't be able to go to Canada. Amabel had said at once that she would much rather be on her own, so her mother had gone, and Amabel had written her a letter each week, giving light-hearted and slightly optimistic accounts of the bed and breakfast business.

Her mother had been gone for a month now; she had phoned when she had arrived and since then had written regularly, although she still hadn't said when she would be returning.

Amabel, considering the matter while Mr Huggett, the church warden, read the first lesson, thought that her mother's next letter would certainly contain news of her return. Not for the world would she admit, even to herself, that she didn't much care for living on her own. She was, in fact, uneasy at night, even though the house was locked and securely bolted.

She kept a stout walking stick which had belonged to her father by the front door, and a rolling pin handy in the kitchen, and there was always the phone; she had only to lift it and dial 999!

Leaving the church presently, and shaking hands with the vicar, she told him cheerfully that her mother would be home very soon.

'You are quite happy living there alone, Amabel? You have friends to visit you, I expect?'

'Oh, yes,' she assured him. 'And there's so much to keep me busy. The garden and the bed and breakfast people keep me occupied.'

He said with vague kindness, 'Nice people, I hope, my dear?'

'I'm careful who I take,' she assured him.

It was seldom that any guests came on a Monday; Amabel cleaned the house, made up beds and checked the fridge, made herself a sandwich and went to the orchard to eat it. It was a pleasant day, cool and breezy, just right for gardening.

She went to bed quite early, tired with the digging, watering and weeding. Before she went to sleep she allowed her thoughts to dwell on Dr Fforde. He seemed like an old friend, but she knew nothing about him. Was he married? Where did he live? Was he a GP, or working at a hospital? He dressed well and drove a Rolls Royce, and he had family or friends somewhere on the other side of Glastonbury. She rolled over in bed and closed her eyes. It was none of her business anyway…

The fine weather held and a steady trickle of tourists knocked on the door. The tea caddy was filling up nicely again; her mother would be delighted. The week slid imperceptibly into the next one, and at the end of it there was a letter from her mother. The postman arrived with it at the same time as a party of four—two couples sharing a car on a brief tour—so that Amabel had to put it in her pocket until they had been shown their rooms and had sat down to tea.

She went into the kitchen, got her own tea and sat down to read it.

It was a long letter, and she read it through to the end—and then read it again. She had gone pale, and drank her cooling tea with the air of someone unaware of what they were doing, but presently she picked up the letter and read it for the third time.

Her mother wasn't coming home. At least not for several months. She had met someone and they were to be married shortly.

I know you will understand. And you'll like him. He's a market gardener, and we plan to set up a garden centre from the house. There's plenty of room and he will build a large glasshouse at the bottom of the orchard. Only he must sell his own market garden first, which may take some months.

It will mean that we shan't need to do bed and breakfast any more, although I hope you'll keep on with it until we get back.

You're doing so well. I know that the tourist season is quickly over but we hope to be back before Christmas.

The rest of the letter was a detailed description of her husband-to-be and news too, of her sister and the baby.

You're such a sensible girl, her mother concluded, *and I'm sure you're enjoying your independence. Probably when we get back you will want to start a career on your own.*

Amabel was surprised, she told herself, but there was no reason for her to feel as though the bottom had dropped out of her world; she was perfectly content to stay at home until her mother and stepfather should return, and it was perfectly natural for her mother to suppose that she would like to make a career for herself.

Amabel drank the rest of the tea, now stewed and cold. She would have plenty of time to decide what kind of career she would like to have.

That evening, her guests in their rooms, she sat down with pen and paper and assessed her accomplishments. She could cook—not quite cordon bleu, perhaps, but to a high standard— she could housekeep, change plugs, cope with basic plumbing. She could tend a garden… Her pen faltered. There was nothing else.

She had her A levels, but circumstances had never allowed her to make use of them. She would have to train for something and she would have to make up her mind what that should be before her mother came home. But training cost money, and she wasn't sure if there would be any. She could get a job and save enough to train…

She sat up suddenly, struck by a sudden thought. Waitresses needed no training, and there would be tips. In one of the larger towns, of course. Taunton or Yeovil? Or what about one of the great estates run by the National Trust? They had shops and tearooms and house guides. The more she thought about it, the better she liked it.

She went to bed with her decision made. Now it was just a question of waiting until her mother and her stepfather came home.

CHAPTER TWO

IT WAS almost a week later when she had the next letter, but before that her mother had phoned. She was so happy, she'd said excitedly; they planned to marry in October—Amabel didn't mind staying at home until they returned? Probably in November?

'It's only a few months, Amabel, and just as soon as we're home Keith says you must tell us what you want to do and we'll help you do it. He's so kind and generous. Of course if he sells his business quickly we shall come home as soon as we can arrange it.'

Amabel had heard her mother's happy little laugh. 'I've written you a long letter about the wedding. Joyce and Tom are giving a small reception for us, and I've planned such a pretty outfit—it's all in the letter...'

The long letter when it arrived was bursting with excitement and happiness.

You have no idea how delightful it is not to have to worry about the future, to have some-one to look after me—you too, of course. Have you decided what you want to do when we get home? You must be so excited at the idea of being independent; you have had such a dull life since you left school...

But a contented one, reflected Amabel. Helping to turn their bed and breakfast business into a success, knowing that she was wanted, feeling that she and her mother were making something of their lives. And now she must start all over again.

It would be nice to wallow in self-pity, but there were two people at the door asking if she could put them up for the night...

Because she was tired she slept all night,

although the moment she woke thoughts came tumbling into her head which were better ignored, so she got up earlier than usual and went outside in her dressing gown with a mug of tea and Cyril and Oscar for company.

It was pleasant sitting on the bench in the orchard in the early-morning sun, and in its cheerful light it was impossible to be gloomy. It would be nice, though, to be able to talk to someone about her future...

Dr Fforde's large, calm person came into her mind's eye; he would have listened and told her what she should do. She wondered what he was doing...

Dr Fforde was sitting on the table in the kitchen of his house, the end one in a short terrace of Regency houses in a narrow street tucked away behind Wimpole Street in London. He was wearing a tee shirt and elderly trousers and badly needed a shave; he had the appearance of a ruffian—a handsome ruffian. There was a half-eaten apple on the table beside him and he was taking great bites from a thick slice of bread and butter. He had been called out just after two o'clock that morning to operate on a patient with a perforated duodenal ulcer; there had been complications which had kept him from his bed and now he was on his way to shower and get ready for his day.

He finished his bread and butter, bent to fondle the sleek head of the black Labrador sitting beside him, and went to the door. It opened as he reached it. The youngish man who came in was already dressed, immaculate in a black alpaca jacket and striped trousers. He had a sharp-nosed foxy face, and dark hair brushed to a satin smoothness.

He stood aside for the doctor and wished him a severe good morning.

'Out again, sir?' His eye fell on the apple core. 'You had only to call me. I'd have got you a nice hot drink and a sandwich…'

The doctor clapped him on the shoulder. 'I know you would, Bates. I'll be down in half an hour for one of your special breakfasts. I disturbed Tiger; would you let him out into the garden?'

He went up the graceful little staircase to his room, his head already filled with thoughts of the day ahead of him. Amabel certainly had no place in them.

Half an hour later he was eating the splendid breakfast Bates had carried through to the small sitting room at the back of the house. Its French windows opened onto a small patio and a garden beyond where Tiger was meandering round. Presently he came to sit by his master, to crunch bacon rinds and then accompany him on a brisk walk through the still quiet streets before the doctor got into his car and drove the short distance to the hospital.

Amabel saw her two guests on their way, got the room ready for the next occupants and then on a sudden impulse went to the village and bought the regional weekly paper at the post office. Old Mr Truscott, who ran it and knew everyone's business, took his time giving her her change.

'Didn't know you were interested in the

Gazette, nothing much in it but births, marriages and deaths.' He fixed her with a beady eye. 'And adverts, of course. Now if anyone was looking for a job it's a paper I'd recommend.'

Amabel said brightly, 'I dare say it's widely read, Mr Truscott. While I'm here I'd better have some more air mail letters.'

'Your ma's not coming home yet, then? Been gone a long time, I reckon.'

'She's staying a week or two longer; she might not get the chance to visit my sister again for a year or two. It's a long way to go for just a couple of weeks.

Over her lunch she studied the jobs page. There were heartening columns of vacancies for waitresses: the basic wage was fairly low, but if she worked full-time she could manage very well... And Stourhead, the famous National Trust estate, wanted shop assistants, help in the tearooms and suitable applicants for full-time work in the ticket office. And none of them were wanted until the end of September.

It seemed too good to be true, but all the same

she cut the ad out and put it with the bed and breakfast money in the tea caddy.

A week went by, and then another. Summer was almost over. The evenings were getting shorter, and, while the mornings were light still, there was the ghost of a nip in the air. There had been more letters from Canada from her mother and future stepfather, and her sister, and during the third week her mother had telephoned; they were married already—now it was just a question of selling Keith's business.

'We hadn't intended to marry so soon but there was no reason why we shouldn't, and of course I've moved in with him,' she said. 'So if he can sell his business soon we shall be home before long. We have such plans...!'

There weren't as many people knocking on the door now; Amabel cleaned and polished the house, picked the last of the soft fruit to put in the freezer and cast an eye over the contents of the cupboards.

With a prudent eye to her future she inspected her wardrobe—a meagre collection of garments, bought with an eye to their long-lasting qualities, in good taste but which did nothing to enhance her appearance.

Only a handful of people came during the week, and no one at all on Saturday. She felt low-spirited—owing to the damp and gloomy weather, she told herself—and even a brisk walk with Cyril didn't make her feel any better. It was still only early afternoon and she sat down in the kitchen, with Oscar on her lap, disinclined to do anything.

She would make herself a pot of tea, write to her mother, have an early supper and go to bed. Soon it would be the beginning of another week; if the weather was better there might be a satisfying number of tourists—and besides, there were plenty of jobs to do in the garden. So she wrote her letter, very bright and cheerful, skimming over the lack of guests, making much of the splendid apple crop and how successful the soft fruit had been. That done, she went on sitting at the kitchen table, telling herself that she would make the tea.

Instead of that she sat, a small sad figure, contemplating a future which held problems. Amabel wasn't a girl given to self-pity, and she couldn't remember the last time she had cried, but she cried now, quietly and without fuss, a damp Oscar on her lap, Cyril's head pressed against her legs. She made no attempt to stop; there was no one there to see, and now that the rain was coming down in earnest no one would want to stop for the night.

Dr Fforde had a free weekend, but he wasn't particularly enjoying it. He had lunched on Saturday with friends, amongst whom had been Miriam Potter-Stokes, an elegant young widow who was appearing more and more frequently in his circle of friends. He felt vaguely sorry for her, admired her for the apparently brave face she was showing to the world, and what had been a casual friendship now bid fair to become something more serious—on her part at least.

He had found himself agreeing to drive her down to Henley after lunch, and once there had been forced by good manners to stay at her friend's home for tea. On the way back to London she had suggested that they might have dinner together.

He had pleaded a prior engagement and gone back to his home feeling that his day had been wasted. She was an amusing companion, pretty and well dressed, but he had wondered once or twice what she was really like. Certainly he enjoyed her company from time to time, but that was all...

He took Tiger for a long walk on Sunday morning and after lunch got into his car. It was no day for a drive into the country, and Bates looked his disapproval.

'Not going to Glastonbury in this weather, I hope, sir?' he observed.

'No, no. Just a drive. Leave something cold for my supper, will you?'

Bates looked offended. When had he ever forgotten to leave everything ready before he left the house?

'As always, sir,' he said reprovingly.

It wasn't until he was driving west through the

quiet city streets that Dr Fforde admitted to himself that he knew where he was going. Watching the carefully nurtured beauty of Miriam Potter-Stokes had reminded him of Amabel. He had supposed, in some amusement, because the difference in the two of them was so marked. It would be interesting to see her again. Her mother would be back home by now, and he doubted if there were many people wanting bed and breakfast now that summer had slipped into a wet autumn.

He enjoyed driving, and the roads, once he was clear of the suburbs, were almost empty. Tiger was an undemanding companion, and the countryside was restful after the bustle of London streets.

The house, when he reached it, looked forlorn; there were no open windows, no signs of life. He got out of the car with Tiger and walked round the side of the house; he found the back door open.

Amabel looked up as he paused at the door. He thought that she looked like a small bedraggled brown hen. He said, 'Hello, may we come in?' and bent to fondle the two dogs, giving her time to wipe her wet cheeks with the back of her hand. 'Tiger's quite safe with Cyril, and he likes cats.'

Amabel stood up, found a handkerchief and blew her nose. She said in a social kind of voice, 'Do come in. Isn't it an awful day? I expect you're on your way to Glastonbury. Would you like a cup of tea? I was just going to make one.'

'Thank you, that would be nice.' He had come into the kitchen now, reaching up to tickle a belligerent Oscar under the chin. 'I'm sorry Tiger's frightened your cat. I don't suppose there are many people about on a day like this—and your mother isn't back yet?'

She said in a bleak little voice, 'No…' and then to her shame and horror burst into floods of tears.

Dr Fforde sat her down in the chair again. He said comfortably, 'I'll make the tea and you shall tell me all about it. Have a good cry; you'll feel better. Is there any cake?'

Amabel said in a small wailing voice, 'But I've been crying and I don't feel any better.' She gave a hiccough before adding, 'And now I've started again.' She took the large white handkerchief he offered her. 'The cake's in a tin in the cupboard in the corner.'

He put the tea things on the table and cut the cake, found biscuits for the dogs and spooned cat food onto a saucer for Oscar, who was still on top of a cupboard. Then he sat down opposite Amabel and put a cup of tea before her.

'Drink some of that and then tell me why you are crying. Don't leave anything out, for I'm merely a ship which is passing in the night, so you can say what you like and it will be forgotten—rather like having a bag of rubbish and finding an empty dustbin…'

She smiled then. 'You make it sound so—so normal…' She sipped her tea. 'I'm sorry I'm behaving so badly.'

He cut the cake and gave her a piece, before saying matter-of-factly, 'Is your mother's absence the reason? Is she ill?'

'Ill? No, no. She's married someone in Canada…'

It was such a relief to talk to someone about it. It all came tumbling out: a hotch-potch of market gardens, plans for coming back and the need for her to be independent as soon as possible.

He listened quietly, refilling their cups, his eyes on her blotched face, and when she had at last finished her muddled story, he said, 'And now you have told me you feel better about it, don't you? It has all been bottled up inside you, hasn't it? Going round inside your head like butter in a churn. It has been a great shock to you, and shocks should be shared. I won't offer you advice, but I will suggest that you do nothing— make no plans, ignore your future—until your mother is home. I think that you may well find that you have been included in their plans and that you need no worries about your future. I can see that you might like to become independent, but don't rush into it. You're young enough to stay at home while they settle in, and that will give you time to decide what you want to do.'

When she nodded, he added, 'Now, go and put your hair up and wash your face. We're going to Castle Cary for supper.'

She gaped at him. ' I can't possibly…'

'Fifteen minutes should be time enough.'

She did her best with her face, and piled her hair neatly, then got into a jersey dress, which was an off the peg model, but of a pleasing shade of cranberry-red, stuck her feet into her best shoes and went back into the kitchen. Her winter coat was out of date and shabby, and for once she blessed the rain, for it meant that she could wear her mac.

Their stomachs nicely filled, Cyril and Oscar were already half asleep, and Tiger was standing by his master, eager to be off.

'I've locked everything up,' observed the doctor, and ushered Amabel out of the kitchen, turned the key in the lock and put it in his pocket, and urged her into the car. He hadn't appeared to look at her at all, but all the same he saw that she had done her best with her appearance. And the restaurant he had in mind had shaded rose lamps on its tables, if he remembered aright…

There weren't many people there on a wet Sunday evening, but the place was welcoming, and the rosy shades were kind to Amabel's still faintly blotchy face. Moreover, the food was good. He watched the pink come back into her cheeks as they ate their mushrooms in garlic sauce, local trout and a salad fit for the Queen. And the puddings were satisfyingly shrouded in thick clotted cream…

The doctor kept up a gentle stream of undemanding talk, and Amabel, soothed by it, was unaware of time passing until she caught sight of the clock.

She said in a shocked voice, 'It's almost nine. You will be so late at Glastonbury…'

'I'm going back to town,' he told her easily, but he made no effort to keep her, driving her back without more ado, seeing her safely into the house and driving off again with a friendly if casual goodbye.

The house, when he had gone, was empty—and too quiet. Amabel settled Cyril and Oscar for the night and went to bed.

It had been a lovely evening, and it had been such a relief to talk to someone about her worries, but now she had the uneasy feeling that she had made a fool of herself, crying and pouring out her problems like a hysterical woman. Because he was a doctor, and was used to dealing with awkward patients, he had listened to her, given her a splendid meal and offered sensible suggestions as to her future. Probably he dealt with dozens like her...

She woke to a bright morning, and around noon a party of four knocked on the door and asked for rooms for the night, so Amabel was kept busy. By the end of the day she was tired enough to fall into bed and sleep at once.

There was no one for the next few days but there was plenty for her to do. The long summer days were over, and a cold wet autumn was predicted.

She collected the windfalls from the orchard, picked the last of the beans for the freezer, saw to beetroots, carrots and winter cabbage and dug the rest of the potatoes. She went to the rickety old greenhouse to pick tomatoes. She supposed that when her stepfather came he would build a new one; she and her mother had made do with it, and the quite large plot they used for vegetables grew just enough to keep them supplied throughout the year, but he was bound to make improvements.

It took her most of the week to get the garden in some sort of order, and at the weekend a party of six stayed for two nights, so on Monday morning she walked to the villager to stock up on groceries, post a letter to her mother and, on an impulse, bought the local paper again.

Back home, studying the jobs page, she saw with regret that the likely offers of work were no longer in it. There would be others, she told herself stoutly, and she must remember what Dr Fforde had told her—not to rush into anything. She must be patient; her mother had said that they hoped to be home before Christmas, but that was still weeks away, and even so he had advised her to do nothing hastily…

It was two days later, while she was putting away sheets and pillowcases in the landing cupboard, when she heard Cyril barking. He sounded excited, and she hurried downstairs; she had left the front door unlocked and someone might have walked in…

Her mother was standing in the hall, and there was a tall thickset man beside her. She was laughing and stooping to pat Cyril, then she looked up and saw Amabel.

'Darling, aren't we a lovely surprise? Keith sold the business, so there was no reason why we shouldn't come back here.'

She embraced Amabel, and Amabel, hugging her back, said, 'Oh, Mother—how lovely to see you.'

She looked at the man and smiled—and knew immediately that she didn't like him and that he didn't like her. But she held out a hand and said, 'How nice to meet you. It's all very exciting, isn't it?'

Cyril had pushed his nose into Keith's hand and she saw his impatient hand push it away. Her heart sank.

Her mother was talking and laughing, looking into the rooms, exclaiming how delightful everything looked. 'And there's Oscar.' She turned to her husband. 'Our cat, Keith. I know you don't like cats, but he's one of the family.'

He made some non-committal remark and went to fetch the luggage. Mrs Parsons, now Mrs Graham, ran upstairs to her room, and Amabel went to the kitchen to get tea. Cyril and Oscar went with her and arranged themselves tidily in a corner of the kitchen, aware that this man with the heavy tread didn't like them.

They had tea in the sitting room and the talk was of Canada and their journey and their plans to establish a market garden.

'No more bed and breakfast,' said Mrs Graham. 'Keith wants to get the place going as soon as possible. If we can get a glasshouse up quickly we could pick up some of the Christmas trade.'

'Where will you put it?' asked Amabel. 'There's plenty of ground beyond the orchard.'

Keith had been out to look around before tea, and now he observed, 'I'll get that ploughed and dug over for spring crops, and I'll put the glasshouse in the orchard. There's no money in apples, and some of the trees look past it. We'll finish picking and then get rid of them. There's plenty of ground there—fine for peas and beans.'

He glanced at Amabel. 'Your mother tells me you're pretty handy around the house and garden. The two of us ought to be able to manage to get something started—I'll hire a man with a rotavator who'll do the rough digging; the lighter jobs you'll be able to manage.'

Amabel didn't say anything. For one thing she was too surprised and shocked; for another, it was early days to be making such sweeping plans. And what about her mother's suggestion that she might like to train for something? If her stepfather might be certain of his plans, but why was he so sure that she would agree to them? And she didn't agree with them. The orchard had always been there, long before she was born. It still produced a good crop of apples and in the spring it was so beautiful with the blossom…

She glanced at her mother, who looked happy and content and was nodding admiringly at her new husband.

It was later, as she was getting the supper that he came into the kitchen.

'Have to get rid of that cat,' he told her briskly.

'Can't abide them, and the dog's getting on a bit, isn't he? Animals don't go well with market gardens. Not to my reckoning, anyway.'

'Oscar is no trouble at all,' said Amabel, and tried hard to sound friendly. 'And Cyril is a good guard dog; he never lets anyone near the house.'

She had spoken quietly, but he looked at her face and said quickly, 'Oh, well, no hurry about them. It'll take a month or two to get things going how I want them.'

He in his turn essayed friendliness. 'We'll make a success of it, too. Your mother can manage the house and you can work full-time in the garden. We might even take on casual labour after a bit—give you time to spend with your young friends.'

He sounded as though he was conferring a favour upon her, and her dislike deepened, but she mustn't allow it to show. He was a man who liked his own way and intended to have it. Probably he was a good husband to her mother, but he wasn't going to be a good stepfather...

Nothing much happened for a few days; there

was a good deal of unpacking to do, letters to write and trips to the bank. Quite a substantial sum of money had been transferred from Canada and Mr Graham lost no time in making enquiries about local labour. He also went up to London to meet men who had been recommended as likely to give him financial backing, should he require it.

In the meantime Amabel helped her mother around the house, and tried to discover if her mother had meant her to have training of some sort and then changed her mind at her husband's insistence.

Mrs Graham was a loving parent, but easily dominated by anyone with a stronger will than her own. What was the hurry? she wanted to know. A few more months at home were neither here nor there, and she would be such a help to Keith.

'He's such a marvellous man, Amabel, he's bound to make a success of whatever he does.'

Amabel said cautiously, 'It's a pity he doesn't like Cyril and Oscar…'

Her mother laughed. 'Oh, darling, he would never be unkind to them.'

Perhaps not unkind, but as the weeks slipped by it was apparent that they were no longer to be regarded as pets around the house. Cyril spent a good deal of time outside, roaming the orchard, puzzled as to why the kitchen door was so often shut. As for Oscar, he only came in for his meals, looking carefully around to make sure that there was no one about.

Amabel did what she could, but her days were full, and it was obvious that Mr Graham was a man who rode roughshod over anyone who stood in his way. For the sake of her mother's happiness Amabel held her tongue; there was no denying that he was devoted to her mother, and she to him, but there was equally no denying that he found Amabel, Cyril and Oscar superfluous to his life.

It wasn't until she came upon him hitting Cyril and then turning on an unwary Oscar and kicking him aside that Amabel knew that she would have to do something about it.

She scooped up a trembling Oscar and bent to put an arm round Cyril's elderly neck. 'How dare you? Whatever have they done to you? They're my friends and I love them,' she added heatedly, 'and they have lived here all their lives.'

Her stepfather stared at her. 'Well, they won't live here much longer if I have my way. I'm the boss here. I don't like animals around the place so you'd best make up your mind to that.'

He walked off without another word and Amabel, watching his retreating back, knew that she had to do something—and quickly.

She went out to the orchard—there were piles of bricks and bags of cement already heaped near the bench, ready to start building the glasshouse—and with Oscar on her lap and Cyril pressed against her she reviewed and discarded several plans, most of them too far-fetched to be of any use. Finally she had the nucleus of a sensible idea. But first she must have some money, and secondly the right opportunity…

As though a kindly providence approved of

her efforts, she was able to have both. That very evening her stepfather declared that he would have to go to London in the morning. A useful acquaintance had phoned to say that he would meet him and introduce him to a wholesaler who would consider doing business with him once he was established. He would go to London early in the morning, and since he had a long day ahead of him he went to bed early.

Presently, alone with her mother, Amabel seized what seemed to be a golden opportunity.

'I wondered if I might have some money for clothes, Mother. I haven't bought anything since you went away…'

'Of course, love. I should have thought of that myself. And you did so well with the bed and breakfast business. Is there any money in the tea caddy? If there is take whatever you want from it. I'll ask Keith to make you an allowance; he's so generous…'

'No, don't do that, Mother. He has enough to think about without bothering him about that; there'll be enough in the tea caddy. Don't bother him.' She looked across at her mother. 'You're very happy with him, aren't you, Mother?'

'Oh, yes, Amabel. I never told you, but I hated living here, just the two of us, making ends meet, no man around the place. When I went to your sister's I realised what I was missing. And I've been thinking that perhaps it would be a good idea if you started some sort of training...'

Amabel agreed quietly, reflecting that her mother wouldn't miss her...

Her mother went to bed presently, and Amabel made Oscar and Cyril comfortable for the night and counted the money in the tea caddy. There was more than enough for her plan.

She went to her room and, quiet as a mouse, got her holdall out of the wardrobe and packed it, including undies and a jersey skirt and a couple of woollies; autumn would soon turn to winter...

She thought over her plan when she was in bed; there seemed no way of improving upon it, so she closed her eyes and went to sleep.

She got up early, to prepare breakfast for her stepfather, having first of all made sure that Oscar and Cyril weren't in the kitchen. Once he had driven away she got her own breakfast, fed both animals and got dressed. Her mother came down, and over her coffee suggested that she might get the postman to give her a lift to Castle Cary.

'I've time to dress before he comes, and I can get my hair done. You'll be all right, love?'

It's as though I'm meant to be leaving, reflected Amabel. And when her mother was ready, and waiting for the postman, reminded her to take a key with her—'For I might go for a walk.'

Amabel had washed the breakfast dishes, tidied the house, and made the beds by the time her mother got into the post van, and if she gave her mother a sudden warm hug and kiss Mrs Graham didn't notice.

Half an hour later Amabel, with Oscar in his basket, Cyril on a lead, and encumbered by her holdall and a shoulder bag, was getting into the taxi she had requested. She had written to her mother explaining that it was high time she became independent and that she would write, but that she was not to worry. *You will both make a great success of the market garden and it will be easier for you both if Oscar, Cyril and myself aren't getting under your feet,* she had ended.

The taxi took them to Gillingham where— fortune still smiling—they got on the London train and, once there, took a taxi to Victoria bus station. By now Amabel realised her plans, so simple in theory, were fraught with possible disaster. But she had cooked her goose. She bought a ticket to York, had a cup of tea, got water for Cyril and put milk in her saucer for Oscar and then climbed into the long-distance bus.

It was half empty, and the driver was friendly. Amabel perched on a seat with Cyril at her feet and Oscar in his basket on her lap. She was a bit cramped, but at least they were still altogether…

It was three o'clock in the afternoon by now, and it was a hundred and ninety-three miles to York, where they would arrive at about half past eight. The end of the journey was in sight, and it only remained for Great-Aunt Thisbe to offer them a roof over their heads. A moot point since she was unaware of them coming…

'I should have phoned her,' muttered Amabel, 'but there was so much to think about in such a hurry.'

It was only now that the holes in her hare-brained scheme began to show, but it was too late to worry about it. She still had a little money, she was young, she could work and, most important of all, Oscar and Cyril were still alive...

Amabel, a sensible level-headed girl, had thrown her bonnet over the windmill with a vengeance.

She went straight to the nearest phone box at the bus station in York; she was too tired and light-headed from her impetuous journey to worry about Great-Aunt Thisbe's reaction.

When she heard that lady's firm, unhurried voice she said without preamble, 'It's me—Amabel, Aunt Thisbe. I'm at the bus station in York.'

She had done her best to keep her voice quiet and steady, but it held a squeak of panic. Supposing Aunt Thisbe put down the phone...

Miss Parsons did no such thing. When she had been told of her dead nephew's wife's remarriage she had disapproved, strongly but silently. Such an upheaval: a strange man taking over from her nephew's loved memory, and what about Amabel? She hadn't seen the girl for some years—what of her? Had her mother considered her?

She said now, 'Go and sit down on the nearest seat, Amabel. I'll be with you in half an hour.'

'I've got Oscar and Cyril with me.'

'You are all welcome,' said Aunt Thisbe, and rang off.

Much heartened by these words, Amabel found a bench and, with a patient Cyril crouching beside her and Oscar eyeing her miserably from the little window in his basket, sat down to wait.

Half an hour, when you're not very happy, can seem a very long time, but Amabel forgot that when she saw Great-Aunt Thisbe walking briskly towards her, clad in a coat and skirt which hadn't altered in style for the last few decades, her white hair crowned by what could best be described as a sensible hat. There was a youngish man with her, short and sturdy with weather-beaten features.

Great-Aunt Thisbe kissed Amabel briskly. 'I

am so glad you have come to visit me, my dear. Now we will go home and you shall tell me all about it. This is Josh, my right hand. He'll take your luggage to the car and drive us home.'

Amabel had got to her feet. She couldn't think of anything to say that wouldn't need a long explanation, so she held out a hand for Josh to shake, picked up Oscar's basket and Cyril's lead and walked obediently out into the street and got into the back of the car while Aunt Thisbe settled herself beside Josh.

It was dark now, and the road was almost empty of traffic. There was nothing to see from the car's window but Amabel remembered Bolton Percy was where her aunt lived, a medieval village some fifteen miles from York and tucked away from the main roads. It must be ten years since she was last here, she reflected; she had been sixteen and her father had died a few months earlier...

The village, when they reached it, was in darkness, but her aunt's house, standing a little apart from the row of brick and plaster cottages near the church, welcomed them with lighted windows.

Josh got out and helped her with the animals and she followed him up the path to the front door, which Great-Aunt Thisbe had opened.

'Welcome to my home, child,' she said. 'And yours for as long as you need it.'

CHAPTER THREE

THE next hour or two were a blur to Amabel; her coat was taken from her and she was sat in a chair in Aunt Thisbe's kitchen, bidden to sit there, drink the tea she was given and say nothing—something she was only too glad to do while Josh and her aunt dealt with Cyril and Oscar. In fact, quite worn out, she dozed off, to wake and find Oscar curled up on her lap, washing himself, and Cyril's head pressed against her knee.

Great-Aunt Thisbe spoke before she could utter a word.

'Stay there for a few minutes. Your room's ready, but you must have something to eat first.'

'Aunt Thisbe—' began Amabel.

'Later, child. Supper and a good night's sleep first. Do you want your mother to know you are here?'

'No, no. I'll explain…'

'Tomorrow.' Great-Aunt Thisbe, still wearing her hat, put a bowl of fragrant stew into Amabel's hands. 'Now eat your supper.'

Presently Amabel was ushered upstairs to a small room with a sloping ceiling and a lattice window. She didn't remember getting undressed, nor did she feel surprised to find both Oscar and Cyril with her. It had been a day like no other and she was beyond surprise or questioning; it seemed quite right that Cyril and Oscar should share her bed. They were still all together, she thought with satisfaction. It was like waking up after a particularly nasty nightmare.

When she woke in the morning she lay for a moment, staring up at the unfamiliar ceiling, but in seconds memory came flooding back and she sat up in bed, hampered by Cyril's weight on her feet and Oscar curled up near him. In the light of early morning yesterday's journey was something unbelievably foolhardy—and she would have to explain to Great-Aunt Thisbe.

The sooner the better.

She got up, went quietly to the bathroom, dressed and the three of them crept downstairs.

The house wasn't large, but it was solidly built, and had been added to over the years, and its small garden had a high stone wall. Amabel opened the stout door and went outside. Oscar and Cyril, old and wise enough to know what was wanted of them, followed her cautiously.

It was a fine morning but there was a nip in the air, and the three of them went back indoors just as Great-Aunt Thisbe came into the kitchen.

Her good morning was brisk and kind. 'You slept well? Good. Now, my dear, there's porridge on the Aga; I dare say these two will eat it. Josh will bring suitable food when he comes presently. And you and I will have a cup of tea before I get our breakfast.

'I must explain…'

'Of course. But over a cup of tea.'

So presently Amabel sat opposite her aunt at

the kitchen table, drank her tea and gave her a carefully accurate account of her journey. 'Now I've thought about it, I can see how silly I was. I didn't stop to think, you see—only that I had to get away because my—my stepfather was going to kill…' She faltered. 'And he doesn't like me.'

'Your mother? She is happy with him?'

'Yes—yes, she is, and he is very good to her. They don't need me. I shouldn't have come here, only I had to think of something quickly. I'm so grateful to you, Aunt Thisbe, for letting me stay last night. I wondered if you would let me leave Oscar and Cyril here today, while I go into York and find work. I'm not trained, but there's always work in hotels and people's houses.'

The sound which issued from Miss Parsons' lips would have been called a snort from a lesser mortal.

'Your father was my brother, child. You will make this your home as long as you wish to stay. As to work—it will be a godsend to me to have someone young about the place. I'm well served by Josh and Mrs Josh, who cleans the place for me, but I could do with company, and in a week or two you can decide what you want to do.

'York is a big city; there are museums, historical houses, a wealth of interest to the visitor in Roman remains—all of which employ guides, curators, helpers of all kinds. There should be choice enough when it comes to looking for a job. The only qualifications needed are intelligence, the Queen's English and a pleasant voice and appearance. Now go and get dressed, and after breakfast you shall telephone your mother.'

'They will want me to go back—they don't want me, but he expects me to work for him in the garden.'

'You are under no obligation to your stepfather, Amabel, and your mother is welcome to come and visit you at any time. You are not afraid of your stepfather?'

'No—but I'm afraid of what he would do to Oscar and Cyril. And I don't like him.'

The phone conversation with her mother wasn't entirely satisfactory—Mrs Graham, at first relieved and glad to hear from Amabel, began to complain bitterly at what she described as Amabel's ingratitude.

'Keith will have to hire help,' she pointed out. 'He's very vexed about it, and really, Amabel, you have shown us a lack of consideration, going off like that. Of course we shall always be glad to see you, but don't expect any financial help—you've chosen to stand on your own two feet. Still, you're a sensible girl, and I've no doubt that you will find work—I don't suppose Aunt Thisbe will want you to stay for more than a week or two.' There was a pause. 'And you've got Oscar and Cyril with you?'

'Yes, Mother.'

'They'll hamper you when you look for work. Really, it would have been better if Keith had had them put down.'

'Mother! They have lived with us for years. They don't deserve to die.'

'Oh, well, but they're neither of them young. Will you phone again?'

Amabel said that she would and put down the

phone. Despite Great-Aunt Thisbe's sensible words, she viewed the future with something like panic.

Her aunt took one look at her face, and said, 'Will you walk down to the shop and get me one or two things, child? Take Cyril with you—Oscar will be all right here—and we will have coffee when you get back.'

It was only a few minutes' walk to the stores in the centre of the village, and although it was drizzling and windy it was nice to be out of doors. It was a small village, but the church was magnificent and the narrow main street was lined with small solid houses and crowned at its end by a large brick and plaster pub.

Amabel did her shopping, surprised to discover that the stern-looking lady who served her knew who she was.

'Come to visit your auntie? She'll be glad of a bit of company for a week or two. A good thing she's spending the winter with that friend of hers in Italy…'

Two or three weeks, decided Amabel, walking

back, should be enough time to find some kind of work and a place to live. Aunt Thisbe had told her that she was welcome to stay as long as she wanted to, but if she did that would mean her aunt would put off her holiday. Which would never do… She would probably mention it in a day or two—especially if Amabel lost no time in looking for work.

But a few days went by, and although Amabel reiterated her intention of finding work as soon as possible her aunt made no mention of her holiday; indeed she insisted that Amabel did nothing about it.

'You need a week or two to settle down,' she pointed out, 'and I won't hear of you leaving until you have decided what you want to do. It won't hurt you to spend the winter here.'

Which gave Amabel the chance to ask, 'But you may have made plans…'

Aunt Thisbe put down her knitting. 'And what plans would I be making at my age, child? Now, let us say no more for the moment. Tell me about your mother's wedding?'

So Amabel, with Oscar on her lap and Cyril sitting between them, told all she knew, and presently they fell to talking about her father, still remembered with love by both of them.

Dr Fforde, immersed in his work though he was, nevertheless found his thoughts wandering, rather to his surprise, towards Amabel. It was some two weeks after she had left home that he decided to go and see her again. By now her mother and stepfather would be back and she would have settled down with them and be perfectly happy, all her doubts and fears forgotten.

He told himself that was his reason for going: to reassure himself that, knowing her to be happy again, he could dismiss her from his mind.

It was mid-afternoon when he got there, and as he parked the car he saw signs of activity at the back of the house. Instead of knocking on the front door he walked round the side of the house to the back. Most of the orchard had disappeared, and there was a large concrete foundation where the trees had been. Beyond the orchard the ground had been ploughed up; the bench had gone, and the fruit bushes. Only the view beyond was still beautiful.

He went to the kitchen door and knocked.

Amabel's mother stood in the doorway, and before she could speak he said, 'I came to see Amabel.' He held out a hand. 'Dr Fforde.'

Mrs Graham shook hands. She said doubtfully, 'Oh, did you meet her when she was doing bed and breakfasts? She's not here; she's left.'

She held the door wide. 'Come in. My husband will be back very shortly. Would you like a cup of tea?'

'Thank you.' He looked around him. 'There was a dog…'

'She's taken him with her—and the cat. My husband won't have animals around the place. He's starting up a market garden. The silly girl didn't like the idea of them being put down—left us in the lurch too; she was going to work for Keith, help with the place once we get started— we are having a big greenhouse built.'

'Yes, there was an orchard there.'

He accepted his tea and, when she sat down, took a chair opposite her.

'Where has Amabel gone?' The question was put so casually that Mrs Graham answered at once.

'Yorkshire, of all places—and heaven knows how she got there. My first husband's sister lives near York—a small village called Bolton Percy. Amabel went there—well, there wasn't anywhere else she could have gone without a job. We did wonder where she was, but she phoned when she got there… Here's my husband.'

The two men shook hands, exchanged a few minutes' conversation, then Dr Fforde got up to go.

He had expected his visit to Amabel's home to reassure him as to her future; it had done nothing of the sort. Her mother might be fond of her but obviously this overbearing man she had married would discourage her from keeping close ties with Amabel—he had made no attempt to disguise his dislike of her.

Driving himself back home, the doctor reflected that Amabel had been wise to leave. It seemed a bit drastic to go as far away as

Yorkshire, but if she had family there they would have arranged her journey. He reminded himself that he had no need to concern himself about her; she had obviously dealt with her own future in a sensible manner. After all, she had seemed a sensible girl...

Bates greeted him with the news that Mrs Potter-Stokes had telephoned. 'Enquiring if you would take her to an art exhibition tomorrow evening which she had already mentioned.'

And why not? reflected Dr Fforde. He no longer needed to worry about Amabel. The art exhibition turned out to be very avant-garde, and Dr Fforde, escorting Miriam Potter-Stokes, listening to her rather vapid remarks, trying to make sense of the childish daubs acclaimed as genius, allowed his thoughts to wander. It was time he took a few days off, he decided. He would clear his desk of urgent cases and leave London for a while. He enjoyed driving and the roads were less busy now.

So when Miriam suggested that he might like to spend the weekend at her parents' home, he declined firmly, saying, 'I really can't spare the time, and I shall be out of London for a few days.'

'You poor man; you work far too hard. You need a wife to make sure that you don't do too much.'

She smiled up at him and then wished that she hadn't said that. Oliver had made some rejoinder dictated by good manners, but he had glanced at her with indifference from cold blue eyes. She must be careful, she reflected; she had set her heart on him for a husband...

Dr Fforde left London a week later. He had allowed himself three days: ample time to drive to York, seek out the village where Amabel was living and make sure that she was happy with this aunt and that she had some definite plans for her future. Although why he should concern himself with that he didn't go into too deeply.

A silly impetuous girl, he told himself, not meaning a word of it.

He left after an early breakfast, taking Tiger with him, sitting erect and watchful beside him, sliding through the morning traffic until at last he reached the M1. After a while he stopped at a service station, allowed Tiger a short run, drank a cup of coffee and drove on until, mindful of Tiger's heavy sighs, he stopped in a village north of Chesterfield.

The pub was almost empty and Tiger, his urgent needs dealt with, was made welcome, with a bowl of water and biscuits, while the doctor sat down before a plate of beef sandwiches, home-made pickles and half a pint of real ale.

Much refreshed, they got back into the car presently, their journey nearing its end. The doctor, a man who, having looked at the map before he started a journey, never needed to look at it again, turned off the motorway and made his way through country roads until he was rewarded by the sight of Bolton Percy's main street.

He stopped before the village stores and went in. The village was a small one; Amabel's whereabouts would be known…

As well as the severe-looking lady behind the counter there were several customers, none of whom appeared to be shopping with any urgency. They all turned to look at him as he went in, and even the severe-looking lady smiled at his pleasant greeting.

An elderly woman at the counter spoke up. 'Wanting to know the way? I'm in no hurry. Mrs Bluett—' she indicated the severe lady '—she'll help you.'

Dr Fforde smiled his thanks. 'I'm looking for a Miss Amabel Parsons.'

He was eyed with even greater interest.

'Staying with her aunt—Miss Parsons up at the End House. End of this street; house stands on its own beyond the row of cottages. You can't miss it. They'll be home.' She glanced at the clock. 'They sit down to high tea around six o'clock, but drink a cup around half past three. Expecting you, is she?'

'No...' Mrs Bluett looked at him so fiercely that he felt obliged to add, 'We have known each other for some time.' She smiled then, and he took his leave, followed by interested looks.

Stopping once more a hundred yards or so down the street, he got out of the car slowly and stood just for a moment looking at the house. It was red brick and plaster, solid and welcoming with its lighted windows. He crossed the pavement, walked up the short path to the front door and knocked.

Miss Parsons opened it. She stood looking at him with a severity which might have daunted a lesser man.

'I have come to see Amabel,' observed the doctor mildly. He held out a hand. 'Fforde—Oliver Fforde. Her mother gave me this address.'

Miss Parsons took his hand and shook it. 'Thisbe Parsons. Amabel's aunt. She has spoken of you.' She looked round his great shoulder. 'Your car? It will be safe there. And a dog?'

She took another good luck at him and liked what she saw. 'We're just about to have a cup of tea. Do bring the dog in—he's not aggressive? Amabel's Cyril is here…'

'They are already acquainted.' He smiled. 'Thank you.'

He let Tiger out of the car and the pair of them followed her into the narrow hallway.

Miss Parsons marched ahead of them, opened

a door and led the way into the room, long and low, with windows at each end and an old-fashioned fireplace at its centre. The furniture was old-fashioned too, beautifully kept and largely covered by photos in silver frames and small china ornaments, some of them valuable, and a quantity of pot plants. It was a very pleasant room, lived in and loved and very welcoming.

The doctor, treading carefully between an occasional table and a Victorian spoon-back chair, watched Amabel get to her feet and heaved a sigh of relief at the pleased surprise on her face.

He said, carefully casual, 'Amabel...' and shook her hand, smiling down at her face. 'I called at your home and your mother gave me this address. I have to be in York for a day or two and it seemed a good idea to renew our acquaintance.'

She stared up into his kind face. 'I've left home...'

'So your stepfather told me. You are looking very well.'

'Oh, I am. Aunt Thisbe is so good to me, and Cyril and Oscar are happy.'

Miss Parsons lifted the teapot. 'Sit down and have your tea and tell me what brings you to York, Dr Fforde. It's a long way from London—you live there, I presume?'

The doctor had aunts of his own, so he sat down, drank his tea meekly and answered her questions without telling her a great deal. Tiger was sitting beside him, a model of canine obedience, while Cyril settled near him. Oscar, of course, had settled himself on top of the bookcase. Presently the talk became general, and he made no effort to ask Amabel how she came to be so far from her home. She would tell him in her own good time, and he had two days before he needed to return to London.

Miss Parsons said briskly, 'We have high tea at six o'clock. We hope you will join us. Unless you have some commitments in York?'

'Not until tomorrow morning. I should very much like to accept.'

'In that case you and Amabel had better take the dogs for a run while I see to a meal.'

It was dark by now, and chilly. Amabel got into

her mac, put Cyril's lead on and led the way out of the house, telling him, 'We can go to the top of the village and come back along the back lane.'

The doctor took her arm and, with a dog at either side of them, they set off. 'Tell me what happened,' he suggested.

His gentle voice would have persuaded the most unwilling to confide in him and Amabel, her arm tucked under his, was only too willing. Aunt Thisbe was a dear, loving and kind under her brusque manner, but she hadn't been there; Dr Fforde had, so there was no need to explain about Cyril and Oscar or her stepfather...

She said slowly, 'I did try, really I did—to like him and stay at home until they'd settled in and I could suggest that I might train for something. But he didn't like me, although he expected me to work for him, and he hated Cyril and Oscar.'

She took a breath and began again, not leaving anything out, trying to keep to the facts and not colouring them with her feelings.

When she had finished the doctor said firmly, 'You did quite right. It was rather hazardous of you to undertake the long journey here, but it was a risk worth taking.'

They were making their way back to the house, and although it was too dark to see he sensed that she was crying. He reminded himself that he had adopted the role of advisor and impersonal friend. That had been his intention and still was. Moreover, her aunt had offered her a home. He resisted a desire to take her in his arms and kiss her, something which, while giving him satisfaction would possibly complicate matters. Instead he said cheerfully, 'Will you spend the afternoon with me tomorrow? We might drive to the coast.'

Amabel swallowed tears. 'That would be very nice,' she told him. 'Thank you.' And, anxious to match his casual friendliness, she added, 'I don't know this part of the world, do you?'

For the rest of the way back they discussed Yorkshire and its beauties.

Aunt Thisbe was old-fashioned; the younger generation might like their dinner in the evening, but she had remained faithful to high tea. The table was elegantly laid, the teapot at one end, a covered dish of buttered eggs at the other, with racks of toast, a dish of butter and a home-made pâté. There was jam too, and a pot of honey, and sandwiches, and in the centre of the table a cake-stand bearing scones, fruitcake, oatcakes and small cakes from the local baker, known as fancies.

The doctor, a large and hungry man, found everything to his satisfaction and made a good meal, something which endeared him to Aunt Thisbe's heart, so that when he suggested he might take Amabel for a drive the following day she said at once that it was a splendid idea. Here was a man very much to her liking; it was a pity that it was obvious that his interest in Amabel was only one of impersonal kindness. The girl had been glad to see him, and heaven knew the child needed friends. A pity that he was only in York for a few days and lived so far away...

He washed the dishes and Amabel dried them after their meal. Aunt Thisbe, sitting in the drawing room, could hear them talking and laughing in the kitchen. Something would have to be done, thought the old lady. Amabel needed young friends, a chance to go out and enjoy herself; life would be dull for her during the winter. A job must be found for her where she would meet other people.

Aunt Thisbe felt sharp regret at the thought of the holiday she would have to forego: something which Amabel was never to be told about.

Dr Fforde went presently, making his goodbyes with beautiful manners, promising to be back the following afternoon. Driving to York with Tiger beside him, he spoke his thoughts aloud. 'Well, we can put our minds at rest, can we not, Tiger? She will make a new life for herself with this delightful aunt, probably find a pleasant job and meet a suitable young man and marry him.' He added, 'Most satisfactory.' So why did he feel so dissatisfied about it?

He drove to a hotel close to the Minster—a Regency townhouse, quiet and elegant, and with the unobtrusive service which its guests took for granted. Tiger, accommodated in the corner of his master's room, settled down for the night, leaving his master to go down to the bar for a nightcap and a study of the city.

The pair of them explored its streets after their breakfast. It was a fine day, and the doctor intended to drive to the coast that afternoon, but exploring the city would give him the opportunity of getting to know it. After all, it would probably be in York where Amabel would find a job.

He lunched in an ancient pub, where Tiger was welcomed with water and biscuits, and then went back to the hotel, got into his car and drove to Bolton Percy.

Amabel had spent the morning doing the small chores Aunt Thisbe allowed her to do, attending to Oscar's needs and taking Cyril for a walk, but there was still time to worry about what she should wear for her outing. Her wardrobe was so scanty that it was really a waste of time to worry about it.

It would have to be the pleated skirt and the short coat she had travelled in; they would pass muster for driving around the country, and Dr Fforde never looked at her as though he actually saw her. It had been lovely to see him again, like meeting an old friend—one who listened without interrupting and offered suggestions, never advice, in the friendliest impersonal manner of a good doctor. He was a doctor, of course, she reminded herself.

He came punctually, spent ten minutes talking to Miss Parsons, suggested that Cyril might like to share the back seat with Tiger, popped Amabel into the car and took the road to the coast.

Flamborough stood high on cliffs above the North Sea, and down at sea level boats sheltered in the harbour. Dr Fforde parked the car, put the dogs on their leads and walked Amabel briskly towards the peninsula. It was breezy, but the air was exhilarating, and they seemed to be the only people around.

When they stopped to look out to sea, Amabel said happily, 'Oh, this is marvellous; so grand and beautiful—fancy living here and waking up each morning and seeing the sea.'

They walked a long way, and as they turned to go back Dr Fforde said, carefully casual, 'Do you want to talk about your plans, Amabel? Perhaps your aunt has already suggested something? Or do you plan to stay with her indefinitely?'

'I wanted to ask you about that. There's a problem. You won't mind if I tell you about it, and perhaps you could give me some advice. You see I was told quite unwittingly, by Mrs Bluett who owns the village shop, that Aunt Thisbe had plans to spend the winter in Italy with a friend. I haven't liked to ask her, and she hasn't said anything, but I can't allow her to lose a lovely holiday like that because I'm here. After all, she didn't expect me, but she's so kind and she might feel that she should stay here so that I've got a home, if you see what I mean.'

They were standing facing each other, and she stared up into his face. 'You can see that I must get a job very quickly, but I'm not sure how to set about it. I mean, should I answer advertisements in the paper or visit an agency? There's not much I can do, and it has to be somewhere Cyril and Oscar can come too.'

He said slowly, 'Well, first you must convince

your aunt that you want a job—and better not say that you know of her holiday. Go to York, put your name down at any agencies you can find…' He paused, frowning. 'What can you do, Amabel?'

'Nothing, really,' she said cheerfully. 'House-work, cooking—or I expect I could be a waitress or work in a shop. They're not the sort of jobs people want, are they? And they aren't well paid. But if I could get a start somewhere, and also somewhere to live…'

'Do you suppose your aunt would allow you to live at her house while she was away?'

'Perhaps. But how would I get to work? The bus service is only twice weekly, and there is nowhere in the village where I could work.' She added fiercely, 'I must be independent.'

He took her arm and they walked on. 'Of course. Now, I can't promise anything, Amabel, but I know a lot of people and I might hear of something. Do you mind where you go?'

'No, as long as I can have Cyril and Oscar with me.'

'There is no question of your returning home?'

'None whatever. I'm being a nuisance to everyone, aren't I?'

He agreed silently to that, but he didn't say so. She was determined to be independent, and for some reason which he didn't understand he wanted to help her.

He asked, 'Have you some money? Enough to pay the rent and so on?'

'Yes, thank you. Mother let me have the money in the tea caddy, and there is still some left.'

He decided it wasn't worth while asking about the tea caddy. 'Good. Now we are going to the village; I noticed a pub as we came through it— the Royal Dog and Duck. If it is open they might give us tea.'

They had a splendid meal in the snug behind the bar: a great pot of tea, scones and butter, cream and jam, great wedges of fruitcake and, in case that wasn't enough, a dish of buttered toast. Tiger and Cyril, sitting under the table, provided with water and any tidbits which came their way, were tired after their walk, and dozed quietly.

He drove back presently through the dusk of

late autumn, taking side roads through charming villages—Burton Agnes, with its haunted manor and Norman church, through Lund, with its once-upon-a-time cockpit, on to Bishop Burton, with its village pond and little black and white cottages, and finally along country roads to Bolton Percy.

The doctor stayed only as long as good manners dictated, although he asked if he might call to wish them goodbye the following morning.

'Come for coffee?' invited Miss Parsons.

The stiff breeze from yesterday had turned into a gale in the morning, and he made that his excuse for not staying long over his coffee. When Amabel had opened the door to him he had handed her a list of agencies in York, and now he wanted to be gone; he had done what he could for her. She had a home, this aunt who was obviously fond of her, and she was young and healthy and sensible, even if she had no looks to speak of. He had no further reason to be concerned about her.

All the same, driving down the M1, he was

finding it difficult to forget her. She had bidden him goodbye in a quiet voice, her small hand in his, wished him a safe journey and thanked him. 'It's been very nice knowing you,' she had told him.

It had been nice knowing her, he conceded, and it was a pity that their paths were unlikely to cross in the future.

That evening Amabel broached the subject of her future to her aunt. She was careful not to mention Aunt Thisbe's holiday in Italy, pointing out with enthusiasm her great wish to become independent.

'I'll never be grateful enough to you,' she assured her aunt, 'for giving me a home—and I love being here with you. But I must get started somewhere, mustn't I? I know I shall like York, and there must be any number of jobs for someone like me—I mean, unskilled labour. And I won't stop at that. You do understand, don't you, Aunt?'

'Yes, of course I do, child. You must go to York and see what there is there for you. Only you must promise me that if you fall on hard times you will come here.' She hesitated, then, 'And if I am not here, go to Josh and Mrs Josh.'

'I promise, Aunt Thisbe. There's a bus to York tomorrow morning, isn't there? Shall I go and have a look round—spy out the land…?'

'Josh has to take the car in tomorrow morning; you shall go with him. The bus leaves York in the afternoon around four o'clock, but if you miss it phone here and Josh will fetch you.'

It was a disappointing day. Amabel went from one agency to the next, and was entered on their books, but there were no jobs which would suit her; she wasn't a trained lady's maid, or a cashier as needed at a café, she had neither the training nor the experience to work at a crêche, nor was she suitable as a saleslady at any of the large stores—lack of experience. But how did one get experience unless one had a chance to learn in the first place?

She presented a brave face when she got back to her aunt's house in the late afternoon. After all, this was only the first day, and her name was down on several agencies' books.

* * *

Back in London, Dr Fforde immersed himself in his work, assuring Bates that he had had a most enjoyable break.

'So why is he so gloomy?' Bates enquired of Tiger. 'Too much work. He needs a bit of the bright lights—needs to get out and about a bit.'

So it pleased Bates when his master told him that he would be going out one evening. Taking Mrs Potter-Stokes to the theatre, and supper afterwards.

It should have been a delightful evening; Miriam was a charming companion, beautifully dressed, aware of how very attractive she was, sure of herself, and amusing him with anecdotes of their mutual friends, asking intelligent questions about his work. But she was aware that she hadn't got his full attention. Over supper she exerted herself to gain his interest, and asked him prettily if he had enjoyed his few days off. 'Where did you go?' she added.

'York…'

'York?' She seized on that. 'My dear Oliver, I wish I'd known; you could have called on a great friend of mine—Dolores Trent. She has one of those shops in the Shambles—you know, sells dried flowers and pots and expensive glass. But she's hopeless at it—so impractical, breaking things and getting all the money wrong. I had a letter from her only a few days ago—she thinks she had better get someone to help her.'

She glanced at the doctor and saw with satisfaction that he was smiling at her. 'How amusing. Is she as attractive as you, Miriam?'

Miriam smiled a little triumphant smile, the evening was a success after all.

Which was what the doctor was thinking…

CHAPTER FOUR

WHEN Amabel came back from walking Cyril the next morning she was met at the door by her aunt.

'A pity. You have just missed a phone call from your nice Dr Fforde. He has heard of a job quite by chance from a friend and thought you might be interested. A lady who owns a shop in the Shambles in York—an arty-crafty place, I gather; she needs someone to help her. He told me her name—Dolores Trent—but he doesn't know the address. You might like to walk through the Shambles and see if you can find her shop. Most thoughtful of him to think of you.'

Josh drove her in after lunch. She was, her aunt had decreed, to spend as long as she wanted in York and phone when she was ready to return; Josh would fetch her.

She walked through the city, found the Shambles and started to walk its length. It was a narrow cobbled street, lined by old houses which overhung the lane, almost all of which were now shops: expensive shops, she saw at once, selling the kind of things people on holiday would take back home to display or give as presents to someone who needed to be impressed.

She walked down one side, looking at the names over the doors and windows, pausing once or twice to study some beautiful garment in a boutique or look at a display of jewellery. She reached the end and started back on the other side, and halfway down she found what she was looking for. It was a small shop, tucked between a bookshop and a mouthwatering patisserie, its small window displaying crystal vases, great baskets of dried silk flowers, delicate china and eye-catching pottery. Hung discreetly in one corner was a small card with 'Shop Assistant Required' written on it.

Amabel opened the door and went inside.

She supposed that the lady who came to meet her through the bead curtain at the back of the shop was Dolores Trent; she so exactly fitted her shop. Miss Trent was a tall person, slightly over-weight, swathed in silky garments and wearing a good deal of jewellery, and she brought with her a cloud of some exotic perfume.

'You wish to browse?' she asked in a casual manner. 'Do feel free…'

'The card in the window?' said Amabel. 'You want an assistant. Would I do?'

Dolores Trent looked her over carefully. A dull little creature, she decided, but quite pleasant to look at, and she definitely didn't want some young glamorous girl who might distract customers from buying.

She said sharply, 'You live here? Have you references? Have you any experience?'

'I live with my aunt at Bolton Percy, and I can get references. I've no experience in working in a shop, but I'm used to people. I ran a bed and breakfast house…'

Miss Trent laughed. 'At least you sound honest. If you come here to work, how will you get here? Bolton Percy's a bit rural, isn't it?'

'Yes. I hope to find somewhere to live here.'

Several thoughts passed with quick succession through Dolores Trent's head. There was that empty room behind the shop, beyond the tiny kitchenette and the cloakroom; it could be furnished with odds and ends from the attic at home. The girl could live there, and since she would have rent-free accommodation there would be no need to pay her the wages she would be entitled to...

Miss Trent, mean by nature, liked the idea.

'I might consider you, if your references are satisfactory. Your hours would be from nine o'clock till five, free on Sundays. I'd expect you to keep the shop clean and dusted, unpack goods when they arrive, arrange shelves, serve the customers and deal with the cash. You'd do any errands, and look after the shop when I'm not here. You say you want to live here? There's a large room behind the shop, with windows and a door opening onto a tiny yard. Basic furniture and bedding. There's a kitchenette and a cloakroom which you can use. Of course you do understand that if I let you live here I won't be able to pay you the usual wages?'

She named a sum which Amabel knew was not much more than half what she should have expected. On the other hand, here was shelter and security and independence.

'I have a dog and a cat. Would you object to them?'

'Not if they stay out of sight. A dog would be quite a good idea; it's quiet here at night. You're not nervous?'

'No. Might I see the room?'

It was a pleasant surprise, quite large and airy, with two windows and a small door opening onto a tiny square of neglected grass. But there were high walls surrounding it; Cyril and Oscar would be safe there.

Dolores Trent watched Amabel's face. The girl needed the job and somewhere to live, so she wasn't likely to leave at a moment's notice if she found the work too hard or the hours too long. Especially with a dog and a cat…

She said, 'Provided your references are okay,

you can come on a month's trial. You'll be paid weekly. After the month it will be a week's notice on either side.' As they went back to the shop she said, 'I'll phone you when I've checked the references.'

Amabel, waiting for Josh to fetch her in answer to her phone call, was full of hope. It would be a start: somewhere to live, a chance to gain the experience which was so necessary if she wanted to get a better job. She would have the chance to look around her, make friends, perhaps find a room where Cyril and Oscar would be welcome, and find work which was better paid. But that would be later, she conceded. In the meantime she was grateful to Dr Fforde for his help. It was a pity she couldn't see him and tell him how grateful she was. But he had disappeared back into his world, somewhere in London, and London was vast…

Convincing Aunt Thisbe that the offer of work from Miss Trent was exactly what she had hoped for was no easy task. Aunt Thisbe had said no word of her holiday, only reiterating her advice that Amabel should spend the next few weeks with her, wait until after Christmas before looking for work…

It was only after Amabel had painted a somewhat overblown picture of her work at Miss Trent's shop, the advantages of getting one foot in the door of future prospects, and her wish to become independent, that Miss Parsons agreed reluctantly that it might be the chance of a lifetime. There was the added advantage that, once in York, the chance of finding an even better job was much greater than if Amabel stayed at Bolton Percy.

So Amabel sent off her references and within a day or so the job was hers, if she chose to take it. Amabel showed her aunt the letter and it was then that Aunt Thisbe said, 'I shall be sorry to see you go, child. You must spend your Sundays here, of course, and any free time you have.' She hesitated. 'If I am away then you must go to Josh and Mrs Josh, who will look after you. Josh will have a key, and you must treat the house as your home. If you need the car you have only to ask…'

'Will you be away for long?' asked Amabel.

'Well, dear, I have been invited to spend a few weeks with an old friend who has an apartment in Italy. I hadn't made up my mind whether to go, but since you have this job and are determined to be independent…'

'Oh, Aunt Thisbe, how lovely for you—and hasn't everything worked out well? I'll be fine in York and I'll love to come here, if Mrs Josh won't mind. When are you going?'

'You are to start work next Monday? I shall probably go during that week.'

'I thought I'd ask Miss Trent if I could move in on Sunday…'

'A good idea. Josh can drive you there and make sure that everything is all right. Presumably the shop will be empty?'

'I suppose so. I'd have all day to settle in, and if it's quiet Cyril and Oscar won't find it so strange. They're very adaptable.'

So everything was settled. Miss Trent had no objection to Amabel moving in on Sunday. The key would be next door at the patisserie, which was open on Sundays, and the room had been furnished; she could go in and out as she wished and she was to be ready to open the shop at nine o'clock on Monday morning. Miss Trent sounded friendly enough, if a trifle impatient.

Amabel packed her case and Miss Parsons, with brisk efficiency, filled a large box with food: tins of soup, cheese, eggs, butter, bread, biscuits, tea and coffee and plastic bottles of milk and, tucked away out of sight, a small radio. Amabel, for all her brave face, would be lonely.

Aunt Thisbe decided that she would put off her holiday until the following week; Amabel would spend Sunday with her and she would see for herself if she could go away with a clear conscience... She would miss Amabel, but the young shouldn't be held back.

She would have liked to have seen the room where Amabel was to live, but she sensed that Amabel didn't want that—at least not until she had transformed it into a place of which her aunt would approve. And there were one or two things she must tell Josh—that nice Dr Fforde might return. It wasn't very likely, but Aunt Thisbe believed that one should never overlook a chance.

Saying goodbye to Aunt Thisbe wasn't easy. Amabel had been happy living with her; she had a real affection for the rather dour old lady, and knew that the affection was reciprocated, but she felt in her bones that she was doing the right thing. Her aunt's life had been disrupted by her sudden arrival and that must not be made permanent. She got into the car beside Josh and turned to smile and wave; she would be back on Sunday, but this was the real parting.

There were few people about on an early Sunday morning: tourists strolling along the Shambles, peering into shop windows, church goers. Josh parked the car away from the city centre and they walked, Amabel with the cat basket and Cyril on his lead, Josh burdened with her case and the box of food.

They knew about her at the patisserie; she fetched the key and opened the shop door, led the way through the shop and opened the door to her new home.

Miss Trent had said that she would furnish it, and indeed there was a divan bed against one wall, a small table by the window with an upright chair, a shabby easy chair by the small electric fire and a worn rug on the wooden floor. There was a pile of bedding and a box of cutlery, and a small table lamp with an ugly plastic shade.

Josh put the box down on the table without saying a word, and Amabel said, too brightly, 'Of course it will look quite different once I've arranged things and put up the curtains.'

Josh said, 'Yes, miss,' in a wooden voice. 'Miss Parsons said we were to go next door and have a cup of coffee. I'll help you sort out your things.'

'I'd love some coffee, but after that you don't need to bother, Josh. I've all the rest of the day to get things how I want. And I must take Cyril for a walk later. There's that park by St Mary Abbot's Church, and then I must take a look round the shop.'

They had their coffee and Josh went away, promising to return on the Sunday morning, bidding her to be sure and phone if she needed him or her aunt. She sensed that he didn't approve of her bid for independence and made haste to assure him that everything was fine…

In her room presently, with the door open and Cyril and Oscar going cautiously around the neglected patch of grass, Amabel paused in her bedmaking to reflect that Miss Trent was certainly a trusting kind of person. 'You would have thought,' said Amabel to Oscar, peering round the open door to make sure that she was there, 'that she would have wanted to make sure that I had come. I might have stolen whatever I fancied from the shop.'

Well, it was nice to be trusted; it augered well for the future…

Dolores Trent had in fact gone to Harrogate for the weekend, with only the briefest of thoughts about Amabel. The girl would find her own way around. It had been tiresome enough finding someone to help out in the shop. Really, she didn't know why she kept the place on. It had been fun when she had first had it, but she hadn't realised all the bookwork there would be, and the tiresome ordering and unpacking…

If this girl needed a job as badly as she had hinted, then she could take over the uninteresting parts and leave Dolores to do the selling. It might even be possible to take more time for herself; the shop was a great hindrance to her social life…

Amabel arranged the odds and ends of furniture to their best advantage, switched on the fire, settled her two companions before it and unpacked the box of food. Aunt Thisbe had been generous and practical. There were tins of soup and a tin opener with them, tins of food for Oscar and Cyril, and there was a fruitcake—one of Mrs Josh's. She stowed them away, together with the other stores, in an empty cupboard she found in the tiny kitchenette.

She also found a saucepan, a kettle, some mugs and plates and a tin of biscuits. Presumably Miss Trent made herself elevenses each morning. Amabel opened a tin of soup and put the saucepan on the gas ring, then went to poke her nose into the tiny cloakroom next to the kitchenette. There was a small geyser over the washbasin; at least there would be plenty of hot water.

She made a list while she ate her soup. A cheap rug for the floor, a pretty lampshade, a couple of cushions, a vase—for she must have flowers—and a couple of hooks so that she could hang her few clothes. There was no cupboard, nowhere to put her undies. She added an orange box to the list, with a question mark behind it. She had no idea when she would have the chance to go shopping. She supposed that the shop would close for the usual half-day during the week, though Miss Trent hadn't mentioned that.

She made Oscar comfortable in his basket, switched off the fire, got Cyril's lead and her coat and left the shop, locking the door carefully behind her. It was mid-afternoon by now, and there was no one about. She walked briskly through the streets to St Mary's, where there was a park, and thought there would be time each morning to take Cyril for a quick run before the shop opened. They could go again after the shop closed. There was the grass for him and Oscar during the day; she could leave the door open...

And there were Sundays to look forward to...

On the way back she wondered about Dr Fforde; she tried not to think about him too often, for that was a waste of time. He had come into her life but now he had gone again. She would always be grateful to him, of course, but she was sensible enough to see that he had no place in it.

When she reached the shop she saw that the patisserie was closing its doors, and presently, when she went to look, the shop lights had been turned out. It seemed very quiet and dark outside, but there were lights here and there above the shops. She took heart from the sight of them.

After she had had her tea she went into the shop, turned on the lights and went slowly from shelf to shelf, not touching but noting their order. She looked to see where the wrapping paper, string and labels were kept, for she felt sure Miss Trent would expect her to know that. She wasn't going to be much use for a few days, but there were some things she would be expected to discover for herself.

She had her supper then, let Oscar and Cyril out for the last time, and got ready for bed. Doing the best she could with a basin of hot water in the cloakroom, she pondered the question of baths—or even showers. The girl at the patisserie had been friendly; she might be able to help. Amabel got into her bed, closely followed by her two companions, and fell instantly asleep.

She was up early—and that was another thing, an alarm clock, she thought as she dressed—opened the door onto the grass patch and then left the shop with Cyril. The streets were empty, save for postmen and milkmen, but there were signs of life when she returned after Cyril's run in the park. The shops were still closed, but curtains were being drawn above them and there was a delicious smell of baking bread from the patisserie.

Amabel made her bed, tidied the room, fed the animals and sat down to her own breakfast—a boiled egg, bread and butter and a pot of tea. Tomorrow, she promised herself, she would buy a newspaper when she went out with Cyril, and, since the patisserie opened at half past eight, she could get croissants or rolls for her lunch.

She tidied away her meal, bade the animals be good and shut and locked the door to the shop. They could go outside if they wanted, and the sun was shining…

She was waiting in the shop when Miss Trent arrived. Beyond a nod she didn't reply to Amabel's good morning, but took off her coat, took out a small mirror and inspected her face.

'I don't always get here as early as this,' she said finally. 'Open the shop if I'm not here, and if I'm not here at lunchtime just close the shop for half an hour and get yourself something. Have you had a look round? Yes? Then put the "Open" sign on the door. There's a feather duster under the counter; dust off the window display then unpack that box under the shelves. Be careful, they are china figures. Arrange them on the bottom shelf and mark the price. That will be on the invoice inside the box.'

She put away the mirror and unlocked the drawer in the counter. 'What was your name?' When Amabel reminded her, she said, 'Yes, well, I shall call you Amabel—and you'd better call me

Dolores. There probably won't be any customers until ten o'clock. I'm going next door for a cup of coffee. You can have yours when I get back.'

Which was half an hour later, by which time Amabel had dealt with the china figures, praying silently that there would be no customers.

'You can have fifteen minutes,' said Dolores. 'There's coffee and milk in the kitchenette; take it into your room if you want to.'

Cyril and Oscar were glad to have her company, even if only for a few minutes, and it made a pleasant break in the morning.

There were people in the shop by now, picking things up and putting them down again, taking their time choosing what they would buy. Dolores sat behind the counter, paying little attention to them and leaving Amabel to wrap up their purchases. Only occasionally she would advise a customer in a languid manner.

At one o'clock she told Amabel to close the door and lock it.

'Open up again in half an hour if I'm not back,' she said. 'Did I tell you that I close on

Wednesday for a half-day? I shall probably go a bit earlier, but you can shut the shop and then do what you like.'

Amabel, while glad to hear about the half-day, thought that her employer seemed rather unbusinesslike. She closed the shop and made herself a sandwich before going to sit on the patch of grass with Oscar and Cyril for company.

She was glad when it was one o'clock on Wednesday; standing about in the shop was surprisingly tiring and, although Dolores was kind in a vague way, she expected Amabel to stay after the shop shut so that she could unpack any new goods or rearrange the windows. Dolores herself did very little, beyond sitting behind the counter holding long conversations over the phone. Only when a customer showed signs of serious buying did she exert herself.

She was good at persuading someone to buy the more expensive glass and china, laughing and chatting in an animated way until the sale was completed, then made no effort to tell Amabel how to go on, seeming content to let her find things out for herself. Amabel supposed that she must make a living from the shop, although it was obvious that she had very little interest in it.

It was a temptation to phone Aunt Thisbe and ask if Josh would fetch her for her half-day, but there were things she wished to do. Shopping for food and material for a window curtain, a new lampshade, flowers… Next week, when she had been paid, she would find a cheerful bedspread for the bed and a cloth for the table.

She did her shopping and took Cyril for a walk, and then spent the rest of her day rearranging her room, sitting by the electric fire eating crumpets for her tea and reading the magazine Dolores had left behind the counter.

Not very exciting, reflected Amabel, but it was early days, and there was Sunday to look forward to. She wrote a letter to her mother, read the magazine from end to end and allowed her thoughts to wander to Dr Fforde.

Sunday came at last, bringing Josh and the prospect of a lovely day and the reality of a warm welcome from Aunt Thisbe.

Warm as well as practical. Amabel was despatched to the bathroom to lie in a pine-scented bath—'For that is something you must miss,' said Miss Parsons. 'Come down when you are ready and we will have coffee and you shall tell me everything.'

Amabel, pink from her bath, settled before the fire in her aunt's drawing room with Oscar and Cyril beside her, and gave a detailed account of her week. She made it light-hearted.

'It's delightful working in such a pleasant place,' she pointed out. 'There are some lovely things in the shop, and Miss Trent—she likes to be called Dolores—is very kind and easygoing.'

'You are able to cook proper meals?'

'Yes, and I do—and the room looks so nice now that I have cushions and flowers.'

'You are happy there, Amabel? Really happy? You have enough free time and she pays you well?'

'Yes, Aunt. York is such a lovely city, and the people in the other shops in the Shambles are so friendly...'

Which was rather an exaggeration, but Aunt

Thisbe must be convinced that there was no reason why she shouldn't go to Italy…

She would go during the following week, Miss Parsons told Amabel, and Amabel was to continue to spend her Sundays at End House; Josh would see to everything…

Amabel, back in her room with another box of food and a duvet her aunt had declared she didn't want, was content that she had convinced the old lady that she was perfectly happy; they would write to each other, and when Aunt Thisbe came back in the New Year they would review the future.

A week or two went by. Amabel bought a winter coat, a pretty cover for the duvet, a basket for Cyril and a cheap rug. She also saved some money—but not much.

After the first two weeks Dolores spent less and less time at the shop. She would pop in at opening time and then go and have her hair done, or go shopping or meet friends for coffee. Amabel found it odd, but there weren't many customers. Trade would pick up again at Christmas, Dolores told her.

Amabel, aware that she was being underpaid and overworked, was nonetheless glad to have her days filled. The few hours she spent in her room once the shop was closed were lonely enough. Later, she promised herself, once she felt secure in her job, she would join a club or go to night school. In the meantime she read and knitted and wrote cheerful letters home.

And when she wasn't doing that she thought about Dr Fforde. Such a waste of time, she told herself. But there again, did that matter? It was pleasant to remember... She wondered what he was doing and wished she knew more about him. Wondered too if he ever thought of her...

To be truthful, he thought of her very seldom; he led a busy life and time was never quite his own. He had driven to Glastonbury once or twice to see his mother, and since the road took him past Amabel's home he had slowed the car to note the work being carried out there. He had thought briefly of calling to see Mrs Graham, but decided against it. There was no point now that Amabel was in York and happy. He hoped that she had settled down by now. Perhaps when he had time to spare he would drive up and go to see her…

He was seeing a good deal of Miriam, and friends were beginning to invite them together to dinner parties. He often spent evenings with her at the theatre when he would much rather have been at home, but she was amusing, and clever enough to appear to have a sincere interest in his work. Hardly aware of it, he was being drawn into her future plans…

It wasn't until one evening, returning home after a long day at the hospital to be met by Bates with a message from Miriam—she—and he— were to join a party of theatregoers that evening, he was to call for her at seven-thirty and after the theatre he would take her out to supper—that he realised what was happening.

He stood for a moment without speaking, fighting down sudden anger, but when he spoke there was nothing of it in his voice.

'Phone Mrs Potter-Stokes, please, and tell her that I am unable to go out this evening.' He smiled suddenly as an idea drowned the anger. 'And, Bates, tell her that I shall be going away.'

There was no expression on Bates's foxy face, but he felt a deep satisfaction. He didn't like Mrs Potter-Stokes and, unlike the doctor, had known for some time that she was set on becoming Mrs Fforde. His 'Very good, Doctor,' was the model of discretion.

As for Dr Fforde, he ate a splendid supper and spent the rest of the evening going through his diary to see how soon he could get away for a couple of days. He would go first to Miss Parsons' house, for Amabel might have chosen to ignore the chance of working in a shop in York. In any case her aunt would know where she was. It would be interesting to meet again…

Almost a week later he set off for York, Tiger beside him. It was a sullen morning, but once he was clear of the endless suburbs the motorway was fairly clear and the Rolls ate up the miles. He stopped for a snack lunch and Tiger's need for a quick trot, and four hours after he had left his home he stopped before Miss Parsons' house.

Of course no one answered his knock, and after a moment he walked down the narrow path beside the house to the garden at the back. It appeared to be empty, but as he stood there Josh came out of the shed by the bottom hedge. He put down the spade he was carrying and walked up the path to meet him.

'Seeking Miss Amabel, are you? House is shut up. Miss Parsons is off to foreign parts for the winter and Miss Amabel's got herself a job in York—comes here of a Sunday; that's her day off.'

He studied the doctor's face. 'You'll want to know where she's working. A fancy shop in the Shambles. Lives in a room at the back with those two animals of hers. Brings them here of a Sunday, spends the day at End House, opens the windows and such, airs the place, has a bath and does her washing and has her dinner with us. Very independent young lady, anxious not to be a nuisance. Says everything is fine at her job but she doesn't look quite the thing, somehow...'

Dr Fforde frowned. 'She got on well with her aunt? They seemed the best of friends...'

'And so they are. I'm not knowing, mind, but I fancy Miss Amabel took herself off so's Miss Parsons didn't have to alter her plans about her holiday.'

'I think you may be right. I'll go and see her, make sure everything is as it should be.'

'You do that, sir. Me and the missus aren't quite easy. But not knowing anyone to talk to about it...'

'I'm here for a day or two, so I'll come and see you again if I may?'

'You're welcome, sir. You and your dog.' Josh bent to stroke Tiger. 'Miss Amabel does know to come here if needful.'

'I'm glad she has a good friend in you, Josh.'

Dr Fforde got back into his car. It was mid afternoon and drizzling; he was hungry, and he must book in at the hotel where he had stayed before, but before doing so he must see Amabel.

She was on her hands and knees at the back of the shop, unpacking dozens of miniature Father Christmases intended for the Christmas market. Dolores was at the hairdresser and would return only in time to lock the till, tell her to close the shop and lock up.

She was tired and grubby, and there hadn't been time to make tea. Dolores expected everything to be cleared away before she got back. At least there had been no customers for a while, but Amabel was becoming increasingly worried at the amount of work Dolores expected her to do. It had been fine for the first few weeks, but Dolores's interest was dwindling. She was in the shop less, and dealing with the customers and sorting out the stock was becoming increasingly difficult. To talk to her about it was risky; she might so easily give Amabel a week's notice, and although she might find work easily enough there were Oscar and Cyril to consider…

She unwrapped the last of the little figures and looked up as someone came into the shop.

Dr Fforde stood in the doorway looking at her. His instant impression was that she wasn't happy, but then she smiled, her whole face alight with pleasure.

He said easily, 'Josh told me where you were. He also told me that Miss Parsons is away.' He glanced round him. 'You live here? Surely you don't run the place on your own?'

She had got to her feet, dusting off her hands, brushing down her skirt.

'No. Dolores—that is, Miss Trent—is at the hairdresser. Are you just passing through?'

'I'm here for a couple of days. When do you close this shop?'

'Five o'clock. But I tidy up after that.'

'Will you spend the evening with me?'

She had bent to stroke Tiger's head. 'I'd like that, thank you. Only I have to see to Oscar and Cyril, and take Cyril for a walk, so I won't be ready until about six o'clock.'

'I'll be here soon after five…'

Dolores came in then, assuming her charming manner at the sight of a customer. 'Have you found something you like? Do take a look round.'

She smiled at him, wondering where he came from; if he was on his own she might suggest showing him what was worth seeing in the city—the patisserie wasn't closed yet...

'I came to see Amabel,' he told her. 'We have known each other for some time, and since I am here for a day or two...'

'You're old friends?' Dolores asked artlessly. 'I expect you know York well? You don't live here?'

'No, but I have been here before. We met some time ago, in the West Country.'

Still artless, Dolores said, 'Oh, I thought you might be from London—I've friends there.' An idea—an unlikely idea—had entered her head. 'But I don't suppose you would know them. I came up here after my divorce, and it was an old schoolfriend—Miriam Potter-Stokes—who persuaded me to do something instead of sitting aimlessly around...'

She knew her wild guess had been successful when he said quietly, 'Yes, I know Miriam. I must tell her how successful you are.'

'Do, please. I must be off. Amabel, close at five o'clock. There'll be a delivery of those candlesticks before nine o'clock tomorrow morning, so be sure to be ready for it.' She gave the doctor a smiling nod. 'Nice to have met you. I hope you enjoy your stay here.'

She wasted no time when she reached her home, but poured herself a drink and picked up the phone.

'Miriam, listen and don't interrupt. Do you know where this Oliver of yours is? You don't? He's a big man, handsome, rather a slow voice, with a black dog? He's in my shop. On the best of terms with Amabel, the girl who works for me. It seems they've known each other for some time.' She gave a spiteful little laugh. 'Don't be too sure that Oliver is yours, Miriam.'

She listened to Miriam's outraged voice, smiling to herself. Miriam was an old schoolfriend, but it wouldn't hurt her to be taken down a peg. Dolores said soothingly, 'Don't get so upset, darling. He's here for a few days; I'll keep an eye on things and let you know if there's anything for you to worry about. Most unlikely, I should think. She's a small dull creature and she wears the most appalling clothes. I'll give you a ring tomorrow some time.'

* * *

When Dolores had gone the doctor said, 'Where do you live, Amabel? Surely not here?'

'Oh, but I do. I have a room behind the shop.'

'You shall show it to me when I come back.' He glanced at his watch. 'In half an hour.'

She said uncertainly, 'Well…'

'You're glad to see me, Amabel?'

She said without hesitating, 'Oh, yes, I am.'

'Then don't dither,' he said.

He came closer, and, looking down into her face, took her hands in his. 'There is a Nigerian proverb which says, "Hold a true friend with both your hands,"' he said. He smiled and added gently, 'I'm your true friend, Amabel.'

CHAPTER FIVE

Closing the shop, tidying up, feeding Oscar and Cyril, doing her face and hair, Amabel was conscious of a warm glow deep inside her person. She had a friend, a real friend. She was going to spend the evening with him and they would talk. There was so much she wanted to talk about…

He had said that he would be back at half past five, so at that time she shut her room door and went back into the shop to let him in, stooping to pat Tiger. 'I still have to take Cyril for a walk,' she told him as she led the way to her room.

He stood in the middle of it, looking round him, absently fondling Cyril. He didn't allow his thoughts to show on his face, but remarked placidly, 'Having access to space for Oscar and

Cyril is an advantage, isn't it? They're happy here with you?'

'Well, yes. It's not ideal, but I'm lucky to have found it. And I have you to thank for that. I couldn't thank you before because I didn't know where you lived.'

'A lucky chance. Can we leave Oscar for a few hours?'

'Yes, he knows I take Cyril out in the evening. I'll get my coat.'

She was longing for a cup of tea; the afternoon had been long and she hadn't had the chance to make one. She was hungry too. He had told her that they were true friends, but she didn't know him well enough to suggest going to a café, and besides, Cyril needed his run.

They set off, talking of nothing much at first, but presently, walking briskly through the park, she began to answer his carefully put questions with equally careful answers.

They had been walking steadily for half an hour when he stopped and caught her by the arm.

'Tea,' he said. 'Have you had your tea? What a thoughtless fool I am.'

She said quickly, 'Oh, it doesn't matter, really it doesn't,' and added, 'It was such a lovely surprise when you came into the shop.'

He turned her round smartly. 'There must be somewhere we can get a pot of tea.'

So she got her tea, sitting at a very small table in a chintzy teashop where shoppers on their way home were still lingering. Since she was hungry, and the doctor seemed hungry too, she tucked into hot buttered toast, hot mince pies and a slice of the delicious walnut cake he insisted that she have.

'I thought we'd have dinner at my hotel,' he told her. 'But if you're not too tired we might take a walk through the streets. York is such a splendid place, and I'd like to know more of it.'

'Oh, so would I. But about going to the hotel for dinner—I think it would be better if I didn't. I mean, there's Cyril, and I'm not—that is—I didn't stop to change my dress.'

'The hotel people are very helpful about dogs.

They'll both be allowed to stay in my room while we dine. And you look very nice as you are, Amabel.'

He sounded so matter-of-fact that her doubts melted away, and presently they continued with their walk.

None of the museums or historical buildings was open, but they wouldn't have visited them anyway; they walked the streets—Lendal Street, Davey Gate, Parliament Street and Coppergate, to stare up at Clifford's Tower, then back through Coppergate and Fosse Gate and Pavement and so to the Shambles again, this time from the opposite end to Dolores's shop. They lingered for a while so that she could show him the little medieval church where she sometimes went, before going on to the Minster, which they agreed would need leisurely hours of viewing in the daylight.

The hotel was close by, and while Amabel went away to leave her coat and do the best she could with her face and hair the doctor went with the dogs. He was waiting for her when she got back to the lounge.

'We deserve a drink,' he told her, 'and I hope you are as hungry as I am.'

It wasn't a large hotel, but it had all the unobtrusive perfection of service and comfort. They dined in a softly lit restaurant, served by deft waiters. The *maître d'* had ushered them to one of the best tables, and no one so much as glanced at Amabel's dowdy dress.

They dined on tiny cheese soufflés followed by roast beef, Yorkshire pudding, light as a feather, crisp baked potatoes and baby sprouts, as gently suggested by the doctor. Amabel looked as though a good meal wouldn't do her any harm, and she certainly enjoyed every mouthful—even managing a morsel of the lemon mousse which followed.

Her enjoyment was unselfconscious, and the glass of claret he ordered gave her face a pretty flush as well as loosening her tongue. They talked with the ease of two people who knew each other well—something which Amabel, thinking about it later, found rather surprising— and presently, after a leisurely coffee, the doctor went to fetch the dogs and Amabel her coat and they walked back to the shop.

The clocks were striking eleven as they reached the shop door. He took the key from her, opened the door and handed her Cyril's lead.

'Tomorrow is Wednesday—you have a half-day?' When she nodded he said, 'Good. Could you be ready by half past one? We'll take the dogs to the sea, shall we? Don't bother with lunch; we'll go next door and have coffee and a roll.'

She beamed up at him. 'Oh, that would be lovely. Dolores almost always goes about twelve o'clock on Wednesdays, so I can close punctually, then there'll only be Oscar to see to.' She added anxiously, 'I don't need to dress up?'

'No, no. Wear that coat, and a scarf for your head; it may be chilly by the sea.'

She offered a hand. 'Thank you for a lovely evening: I have enjoyed it.'

'So have I.' He sounded friendly, and as though he meant it—which of course he did. 'I'll wait until you're inside and locked up. Goodnight, Amabel.'

She went through the shop and turned to lift a hand to him as she opened the door to her room and switched on the light. After a moment he went back to his hotel. He would have to return to London tomorrow, but he could leave late and travel through the early part of the night so that they could have dinner together again.

'Am I being a fool?' he enquired of Tiger, whose gruff rumble could have been either yes or no...

It was halfway through the busy morning when Dolores asked casually, 'Did you have a pleasant evening with your friend, Amabel?'

Amabel warmed to her friendly tone. 'Oh, yes, thank you. We went for a walk through the city and had dinner at his hotel. And this afternoon we're going to the sea.'

'I dare say you found plenty to talk about?'

'Yes, yes, we did. His visit was quite unexpected. I really didn't expect to see him again...'

'Does he come this way often? It's quite a long journey from London.'

'Well, yes. He came just before I started work

here—my mother told him where I was and he looked me up.'

She had answered readily enough, but Dolores was prudent enough not to ask any more questions. She said casually, 'You must wrap up; it will be cold by the sea. And you can go as soon as he comes for you; I've some work I want to do in the shop.'

She's nicer than I thought, reflected Amabel, going back to her careful polishing of a row of silver photo frames.

Sure enough, when the doctor's large person came striding towards the shop, Dolores said, 'Off you go, Amabel. He can spend ten minutes in the shop while you get ready.'

While Amabel fed Oscar, got Cyril's lead and got into her coat, tidied her hair and made sure that she had everything in her handbag, Dolores invited the doctor to look round him. 'We're showing our Christmas stock,' she told him. 'It's always a busy time, but we close for four days over the holiday. Amabel will be able to go to her aunt's house. She's away at present, Amabel told me, but I'm sure she'll be back by then.' She gave him a sly glance. 'I dare say you'll manage to get a few days off?'

'Yes, I dare say.'

'Well, if you see Miriam give her my love, won't you? Are you staying here long?'

'I'm going back tonight. But I intend to return before Christmas.'

Amabel came then, with Cyril on his lead. She looked so happy that just for a moment Dolores had a quite unusual pang of remorse. But it was only a pang, and the moment they had gone she picked up the phone.

'Miriam—I promised to ring you. Your Oliver has just left the shop with Amabel. He's driving her to the sea and spending the rest of the day with her. What is more, he told me that he intends returning to York before Christmas. You had better find yourself another man, darling!'

She listened to Miriam raging for a few minutes. 'I shouldn't waste your breath getting into a temper. If you want him as badly as all that then you must think of something. When you have, let me know if I can help.'

Miriam thought of something at once. When Dolores heard it she said, 'Oh, no, I can't do that.' For all her mischief-making she wasn't deliberately unkind. 'The girl works very well, and I can't just sack her at a moment's notice.'

'Of course you can; she's well able to find another job—plenty of work around before Christmas. When he comes tell Oliver she's found a better job and you don't' know where it is. Tell him you'll let him know if you hear anything of her; he won't be able to stay away from his work for more than a couple of days at a time. The girl won't come to any harm, and out of sight is out of mind...'

Miriam, most unusually for her burst into tears, and Dolores gave in; after all, she and Miriam were very old friends...

The doctor and his little party had to walk to where he had parked the car, and on the way he marshalled them into a small pub in a quiet street to lunch upon a sustaining soup, hot crusty bread and a pot of coffee—for, as he explained, they couldn't walk on empty stomachs. That done, he drove out of the city, north through the Yorkshire Moors, until he reached Staithes, a fishing village between two headlands.

He parked the car, tucked Amabel's hand under his arm and marched her off into the teeth of a strong wind, the dogs trotting happily on either side of them. They didn't talk; the wind made that difficult and really there was no need. They were quite satisfied with each other's company without the need of words.

The sea was rough, grey under a grey sky, and once away from the village there was no one about. Presently they turned round, and back in the village explored its streets. The houses were a mixture of cottages and handsome Georgian houses, churches and shops. They lingered at the antiques shops and the doctor bought a pretty little plate Amabel admired before they walked on beside the Beck and finally turned back to have tea at the Cod and Lobster pub.

It was a splendid tea; Amabel, her cheeks pink,

her hair all over the place and glowing with the exercise, ate the hot buttered parkin, the toast and home-made jam and the fruit cake with a splendid appetite.

She was happy—the shop, her miserable little room, her loneliness and lack of friends didn't matter. Here she was, deeply content, with someone who had said that he was her friend.

They didn't talk about themselves or their lives; there were so many other things to discuss. The time flew by and they got up to go reluctantly.

Tiger and Cyril, nicely replete with the morsels they had been offered from time to time, climbed into the car, went to sleep and didn't wake until they were back in York. The doctor parked the car at his hotel, led the dogs away to his room and left Amabel to tidy herself. It was no easy task, and she hardly felt at her best, but it was still early evening and the restaurant was almost empty.

They dined off chicken *à la king* and lemon tart which was swimming in cream, and the doctor talked comfortably of this and that. Amabel wished that the evening would go on for ever.

It didn't of course. It was not quite nine o'clock when they left the hotel to walk back to the shop. The girl who worked in the patisserie was still there, getting ready to leave. She waved as they passed and then stood watching them. She liked Amabel, who seemed to lead a very dull and lonely life, and now this handsome giant of a man had turned up...

The doctor took the key from Amabel, opened the shop door and then gave it back to her.

'Thank you for a lovely afternoon—Oliver. I feel full of fresh air and lovely food.'

He smiled down at her earnest face. 'Good. We must do it again, some time. When she looked uncertain, he added, 'I'm going back to London tonight, Amabel. But I'll be back.'

He opened the door and pushed her inside, but not before he had given her a quick kiss. The girl in the patisserie saw that, and smiled. Amabel didn't smile, but she glowed from the top of her head to the soles of her feet.

He had said that he would come back...

* * *

Dolores was in a friendly mood in the morning; she wanted to know where Amabel had gone, if she had had a good dinner, and was her friend coming to see her again?

Amabel, surprised at the friendliness, saw no reason to be secretive. She gave a cheerful account of her afternoon, and when Dolores observed casually, 'I dare say he'll be back again?' Amabel assured her readily enough that he would.

Any niggardly doubts Dolores might have had about Miriam's scheme were doused by the girl in the patisserie who served her coffee.

'Nice to see Amabel with a man,' she observed chattily. 'Quite gone on her, I shouldn't doubt. Kissed her goodbye and all. Stood outside the shop for ages, making sure she was safely inside. He'll be back, mark my words! Funny, isn't it? She's such a plain little thing, too…'

This was something Miriam had to know, so Dolores sent Amabel to the post office to collect a parcel and picked up the phone.

She had expected rage, perhaps tears from

Miriam, but not silence. After a moment she said, 'Miriam?'

Miriam was thinking fast; the girl must be got rid of, and quickly. Any doubts Dolores had about that must be quashed at once. She said in a small broken voice, 'Dolores, you must help me. I'm sure it's just a passing in-fatuation—only a few days ago we spent the evening together.' That there wasn't an atom of truth in that didn't worry her; she had to keep Dolores's sympathy.

She managed a sob. 'If he goes back to see her and she's gone he can't do anything about it. I know he's got commitments at the hospital he can't miss.' Another convincing lie. 'Please tell him that she's got another job but you don't know where? Or that she's got a boyfriend? Better still tell him that she said she would join her aunt in Italy. He wouldn't worry about her then. In fact that's what she will probably do...'

'That cat and dog of hers—' began Dolores.

'Didn't you tell me that there was a kind of

handyman who does odd jobs for the aunt? They'll go to him.'

Put like that, it sounded a reasonable solution. 'You think she might do that?' Dolores was still doubtful, but too lazy to worry about it. She said, 'All right, I'll sack her—but not for a day or two. There's more Christmas stock to be unpacked and I can't do that on my own.'

Miriam gave a convincing sob. 'I'll never be able to thank you enough. I'm longing to see Oliver again; I'm sure everything will be all right once he's back here and I can be with him.'

Which was unduly optimistic of her. Oliver, once back home, made no attempt to contact her. When she phoned his house it was to be told by a wooden-voiced Bates that the doctor was unavailable.

In desperation she went to his consulting rooms, where she told his receptionist that he was expecting her when he had seen his last patient, and when presently he came into the waiting room from his consulting room she went to meet him.

'Oliver—I know I shouldn't be here. Don't

blame your receptionist; I said you expected me. Only it is such a long time since we saw each other.'

She lifted her faced to his, aware that she was at her most attractive. 'Have I done something to annoy you? You are never at home when I phone; that man of yours says you're not available.' She put a hand on his sleeve and smiled the sad little smile she had practised before her mirror.

'I've been busy—am still. I'm sorry I haven't been free to see you, but I think you must cross me off your list, Miriam.' He smiled at her. 'I'm sure there are half a dozen men waiting for the chance to take you out.'

'But they aren't you, Oliver.' She laughed lightly. 'I don't mean to give you up, Oliver.' She realised her mistake when she saw the lift of his eyebrows, and added quickly, 'You are a perfect companion for an evening out, you know.'

She wished him a light-hearted goodbye then, adding, 'But you'll be at the Sawyers' dinner party, won't you? I'll see you then.'

'Yes, of course.' His goodbye was friendly, but

she was aware that only good manners prevented him from showing impatience.

The sooner Dolores got rid of that girl the better, thought Miriam savagely. Once she was out of the way she would set about the serious business of capturing Oliver.

But Dolores had done nothing about sacking Amabel. For one thing she was too useful at this busy time of the year, and for another Dolores's indolence prevented her from making decisions. She was going to have to do something about it, because she had said she would, but later.

Then an ill-tempered and agitated phone call from Miriam put an end to indecision. A friend of Miriam's had mentioned casually that it was a pity that Oliver would be away for her small daughter's—his goddaughter's—birthday party. He'd be gone for several days, he had told her. The birthday was in three days' time…

'You must do something quickly—you promised.' Miriam managed to sound desperately unhappy, although what she really felt was rage. But it wouldn't do to lose Dolores's sympathy. She gave a sob. 'Oh, my dear, I'm so unhappy.'

And Dolores, her decision made for her, promised. 'The minute I get to the shop in the morning.'

Amabel was already hard at work, unwrapping Christmas tree fairies, shaking out their gauze wings and silky skirts, arranging them on a small glass shelf. She wished Dolores good morning, the last of the fairies in her hand.

Dolores didn't bother with good morning. She disliked unpleasantness if it involved herself, and the quicker it was dealt with the better.

'I'm giving you notice,' she said, relieved to find that once she had said it it wasn't so difficult. 'There's not enough work for you, and besides, I need the room at the back. You can go this evening, as soon as you've packed up. Leave your bits and pieces; someone can collect them. You'll get your wages, of course.'

Amabel put the last fairy down very carefully on the shelf. Then she said in a small shocked voice, 'What have I done wrong?'

Dolores picked up a vase and inspected it carefully. 'Nothing. I've just told you; I want the room and I've no further use for you in the shop.' She looked away from Amabel. 'You can go back to your aunt, and if you want work there'll be plenty of casual jobs before Christmas.'

Amabel didn't speak. Of what use? Dolores had made herself plain enough; to tell her that her aunt was still away, and that she had had a card from Josh that morning saying that he and Mrs Josh would be away for the next ten days and would she please not go and visit them as usual next Sunday, would be useless.

Dolores said sharply, 'And it's no use saying anything. My mind's made up. I don't want to hear another word.'

She went to the patisserie then, to have her coffee, and when she came back told Amabel that she could have an hour off to start her packing.

Amabel got out her case and began to pack it, explaining to Cyril and Oscar as she did so. She had no idea where she would go; she had enough money to pay for a bed and breakfast place, but would they take kindly to the animals? There wouldn't be much time to find somewhere once she left the shop at five o'clock. She stripped the bed, packed what food she had in a box and went back to the shop.

When five o'clock came Dolores was still in the shop.

She gave Amabel a week's wages, told her that she could give her name for a reference if she needed to, and went back to sit behind the counter.

'Don't hang about,' she said. 'I want to get home.'

But Amabel wasn't going to hurry. She fed Oscar and Cyril and had a wash, made a cup of tea and a sandwich, for she wasn't sure where the next meal would come from, and then, neatly dressed in her new winter coat, with Cyril on his lead, Oscar in his basket and carrying her case, she left the shop.

She didn't say anything. Good evening would have been a mockery; the evening was anything but good. She closed the shop door behind her, picked up her case, waved to the girl in the patisserie, and started off at a brisk pace, past the still lighted shops.

She didn't know York well, but she knew that she wasn't likely to find anywhere cheap in and around the main streets. If she could manage until Josh and his wife got back…

She reached the narrow side streets and presently saw a café on a street corner. It was a shabby place, but it had a sign in its window saying 'Rooms to Let'. She went inside and went to the counter, where a girl lounged reading a magazine.

The place was almost empty; it smelled of fried food and wasn't too clean, but to Amabel it was the answer to her prayers.

The girl was friendly enough. Yes, there was a room, and she could have it, but she didn't know about the dog and cat. She went away to ask and came back to say that there was a room on the ground floor where the animals could stay with her, but only at night; during the day she would have to take them with her. 'And since we're doing you a favour we'll have to charge more.'

A lot more. But at least it was a roof over their heads. It was a shabby roof, and a small ill-furnished room, but there was a wash handbasin and a window opening onto a window box which had been covered by wire netting, and that solved Oscar's problems.

Amabel handed over the money, left her case, locked the door and went out again, intent on finding a cafeteria. Presently, feeling all the better for a meal, still accompanied by Oscar in his basket and Cyril, she bought a take away meat pie and milk, carrying them to her room.

Oscar, let out of his basket at last, made a beeline for the window box, and then settled down to eat the meat in the pie while Cyril wolfed the crust, washing it down with the milk before climbing onto the bed.

Amabel washed in tepid water, cleaned her teeth, got into her nightie and then into bed. She was tired, too tired to think rationally, so she closed her eyes and went to sleep.

She was up early, asked for tea and toast from the girl at the counter and took Cyril out for five minutes. Since she didn't dare to leave Oscar he went too, grumbling in his basket.

Assuring the girl they would be back in the evening, she locked the door and set off into the cold bright morning.

It was apparent by midday that a job which would admit Cyril and Oscar was going to be hard to find. Amabel bought a carton of milk and a ham roll and found a quiet corner by St Mary's, where she fed Oscar and Cyril from the tin she had in her shoulder bag before letting a timid Oscar out to explore the flowerbeds. With a cat's good sense he stayed close to her, and soon got back into his basket and settled down again. He was a wise beast and he was aware that they were, the three of them, going through a sticky patch...

The afternoon was as disappointing as the morning, and the café, when Amabel got back to it, looked uninviting. But it spelled security of a sort, and tomorrow was another day.

Which turned out to be most unfortunately, just like the previous one. The following

morning, when Amabel went to her frugal breakfast in the café, the girl at the counter leaned
across to say, 'Can't put you up any longer. Got
a regular booked the room for a week.'

Amabel chewed toast in a dry mouth. 'But
there's another room I can rent?'

'Not with them animals. Be out by ten o'clock,
will you? So's I can get the bed changed.'

'But just for a few nights?'

'Not a hope. The boss turned a blind eye for a
couple of nights but that's it. Tried the Salvation
Army, have you? There's beds there, but you'd
have to find somewhere for that dog and cat.'

It was another fine morning, but cold. Amabel
found a sheltered seat in the park and sat down
to think. She discarded the idea of going home.
She had escaped once; it might not be as easy
again, and nothing was going to make her
abandon Cyril and Oscar.

It was a question of waiting for eight days
before Josh and his wife returned, and, however
careful she was, there wasn't enough money in
her purse to buy them bed and board for that

time. She would try the Salvation Army—after five o'clock the girl had said—and hope that they would allow Cyril and Oscar to stay with her.

She had bought a local paper, so now she scanned the vacancies in the jobs columns. She ticked off the most promising, and set off to find the first of them. It was a tiresome business, for her suitcase was quite heavy and Oscar's basket got in the way. Each time she was rejected. Not unkindly, but with an indifference which hurt.

It was after four o'clock when she finally gave up and started on her way to the Salvation Army shelter. She had to pass the end of the Shambles to reach it, and on an impulse she turned aside and went through the half-open door of the little church she had sometimes visited. It was quiet inside and there was no one there. It was cold too, and dimly lighted, but there was peace there…

Amabel sat down in one of the old-fashioned high-backed pews, put Oscar's basket beside her, and, with her case on the other side and Cyril at her feet, allowed the tranquillity of the little church to soothe her.

She said aloud, 'Things are never as bad as they seem,' and Cyril thumped his tail in agreement. Presently, tired from all the walking, he went to sleep. So did Oscar, but Amabel sat without moving, trying to make plans in her tired head which, despite her efforts, was full of thoughts of Oliver. If he were there, she thought dreamily, he would know exactly what to do…

The doctor had reached York shortly after lunch, booked a room at the hotel and, with the faithful Tiger loping beside him, made his way to Dolores's shop. She was sitting behind the counter, reading, but she looked up as he went in and got to her feet. She had known that sooner or later he would come, but she still felt a momentary panic at the sight of him. Which was silly of her; he stood there in the doorway, large and placid, and his quiet greeting was reassuring.

'I've come to see Amabel,' he told her. 'Will you allow her to have an hour or two off? Or perhaps the rest of the afternoon? I can't stay in York long…'

'She's not here…'

'Oh, not ill, I hope?'

'She's gone. I didn't need her any more.' There was no expression on his face, but she took a step backwards. 'She's got an aunt to go to.'

'When was this? She had a week's notice, presumably?'

Dolores picked up a vase on the counter and put it down again. She said again, 'There's this aunt…'

'You sent her packing at a moment's notice?' The doctor's voice was quiet, but she shivered at the sound of it. 'She took the cat and dog with her?'

'Of course she did.'

'Did you know that her aunt was away from home?'

Dolores shrugged. 'She did mention it.' She would have to tell him something to make him see that it was useless looking for the girl. 'Amabel said something about going to stay with friends of her mother—somewhere near…' She paused for a moment, conjuring up names out of the back of her head. 'I think she said Nottingham—a Mrs Skinner…'

She heaved a sigh of relief; she had done that rather well.

He stood looking at her, his face inscrutable, his eyes cold. 'I don't believe you. And if any harm comes to Amabel I shall hold you responsible.'

He left the shop, closing the door quietly behind him, and Dolores flew to the kitchenette and reached for the bottle of whisky she kept hidden away there. Which meant that she missed seeing the girl at the patisserie go to the door and call to the doctor.

'Hi—you looking for Amabel? Poor kid got the sack at a moment's notice—told she wasn't wanted by that Dolores, I suppose...'

'You spoke to her?'

'Didn't have a chance. Had me hands full of customers. She waved though—had her case and that dog and cat, going heaven knows where. Haven't seen hair nor hide of her since...'

'How long ago?'

'Two days?'

'Dolores said that she had gone away to friends.'

The girl sniffed. 'Don't you believe it—that

woman will tell you anything she thinks you want to hear.'

'Yes. You think Amabel is still in York? I'm going to drive to her aunt's house now; there's a man, Josh…'

'I've seen 'im once or twice of a Sunday—brings her back here—she goes there on her free day.'

The doctor thanked her. 'Probably she is there—and thank you. I'll let you know if I find her.'

'You do that—I liked her.'

She watched him go. He was a man to satisfy any girl's dreams, not to mention the money. That was a cashmere coat, and a silk tie costing as much as one of her dresses…

Of course there was no one at Miss Parsons' house, and no response from Josh's cottage when he knocked. He was equally unsuccessful at the village shop—Josh was away, he was told, and there had been no sign of Amabel.

The doctor drove back to York, parked the car once more at the hotel and set off with Tiger to scour the city. He was worried, desperately concerned as to Amabel's whereabouts. He forced himself to think calmly as he systematically combed the streets of the inner city.

He didn't believe for one moment that Amabel had left York, and he thought it unlikely that she would have had enough money to get her home. And to go home was the most unlikely thing she would do. She was here, still in York. It was just a question of finding her...

He stopped at several of the smaller shops to ask if anyone had seen her and was told in one of them—a shabby little café—that there had been a girl with a dog. She had bought a roll and had coffee two days ago. A slender clue, but enough to take the doctor through the streets once more.

It was as he reached the lower end of the Shambles for the second time that his eye lighted on the little church close by. He remembered then that Amabel had told him that she had gone there from time to time. He went through its open door and stood just inside, aware of the quiet and the cold, and he saw Amabel, a small vague figure in the distance.

He heaved a great sigh and went quietly to

where she was sitting. 'Hello, Amabel,' he said in a calm voice, 'I thought I might find you here.'

She turned her head slowly as Cyril got to his feet, wagging his tail and whining with pleasure. 'Oliver—Oliver, is it really you?'

She stopped because she was crying, and he went and sat down beside her and put a great arm around her shoulders. He sat quietly and let her weep, and when her sobs became sniffs offered a handkerchief.

'So sorry,' said Amabel. 'You were a surprise—at least, I was thinking about you, and there you were.'

He was relieved to hear that her voice, while still watery, was quite steady.

'Are you staying in York?' she asked politely. 'It's nice to see you again. But don't let me keep you.'

The doctor choked back a laugh. Even in dire circumstances, Amabel, he felt sure, would always be polite. He said gently, 'Amabel, I went to the shop and that woman—Dolores—told me what she had done. I've spent hours looking for you, but we aren't going to talk about it now. We are going to the hotel, and after a meal and a good night's sleep we will talk.'

'No,' said Amabel quite forcibly. 'I won't. What I mean is, thank you, but no. Tomorrow…'

He had Oscar's basket, and her case. Now he said, 'One day at a time, Amabel.'

CHAPTER SIX

SEVERAL hours later Amabel, fed and bathed and in bed, with Cyril curled up on the floor and Oscar stretched out on her feet, tried to sort out the evening so that it made sense. As it was, it had been a fairy tale dream. In no other way could she account for the last few hours.

How had Oliver been able to conjure a private sitting room out of thin air? A tray of tea, food for Oscar and Cyril? Her case had been unpacked and its contents whisked away to be washed and pressed, she was in a bedroom with a balcony where Oscar could feel free, had had a delicious meal and a glass of wine, and Oliver urging her to eat and drink and not ask questions but to go to bed since they must leave early in the morning.

She had obeyed sleepily, thanked him for her

supper and said goodnight, then spent ages in the bath. And it had all seemed perfectly normal—just as a dream was always normal. In the morning she must find a way of leaving, but now she would just close her eyes…

She opened them to thin sunshine through the drawn curtains and a cheerful girl with a tray of tea.

'Dr Fforde asks that you dress quickly and meet him in the sitting room in twenty minutes—and I'm to take the dog with me so that he can have a run with the doctor's dog.'

Amabel drank her tea, put Oscar on the balcony and went into the sitting room. She showered and dressed with all speed, anxious not to keep Oliver waiting, so her hair didn't look its best and her make-up was perfunctory, but she looked rested and ready for anything.

The doctor was at a window, looking out onto the street below. He turned round as she went in and studied her. 'That's better. You slept well?'

'Yes. Oh, yes, I did. It was like heaven.' She bent to stroke Cyril's head. 'Thank you for taking him out. And thank you for letting me stay here. It's like a dream.'

Breakfast was brought in then, and when they had sat down at the table she said, 'I expect you are in a hurry. The maid asked me to be quick. I'm very grateful, Oliver, for your kindness.' She added, 'There are several jobs I shall go and see about this morning.'

The doctor loaded toast with marmalade. 'Amabel, we are friends, so let us not talk nonsense to each other. You are a brave girl, but enough is enough. In half an hour or so we are leaving York. I have written to Josh so that he will know what has happened when he comes back home, and we will let Miss Parsons know as soon as possible.'

'Know what?'

'Where you will be and what you will be doing.'

'I'm not going home.'

'No, no, of course not. I am hoping that you will agree to do something for me. I have a great-aunt recovering from a slight stroke. Her one wish is to return to her home, but my mother hasn't been able to find someone who will live with her for a time. No nursing is needed, but a willingness to talk and be talked to, join in any small amusement she may fancy, help her to make life enjoyable. She is old, in her eighties, but she loves her garden and her home. She has a housekeeper and a housemaid who have both been with her for years. And don't think that I'm asking you to do this because you happen to be between jobs...'

Which sounded so much better, reflected Amabel, than being out of work, or even destitute. He was asking for her help and she owed him a great deal. Besides, he was her friend, and friends help each other when they were needed.

She said, 'If your great-aunt would like me to be with her, then I'll go to her. But what about Cyril and Oscar?'

'She has a house in the country; she likes animals and they will be welcome there. I should point out that she is a very old lady and liable to have another stroke, so the prospect for you is not a permanent one.'

Amabel drank the last of her coffee. 'Well, I expect for someone like me, with no special skills, it would be hard to find permanent work. But I must write to Aunt Thisbe and tell her.'

'Better still, if you have her phone number you can ring her up.'

'May I? When we get to wherever we are going?'

He crossed the room to the telephone on a side table. 'You have the number with you?' He held out a hand and she handed him the grubby slip of paper she had carried everywhere with her. He got the receptionist and waited for her to get the number, then handed Amabel the phone.

Aunt Thisbe's voice was loud and clear, demanding to know who it was.

'It's me. Amabel. There's nothing wrong, but I must tell you—that is, I must explain—'

The phone was taken from her. 'Miss Parsons? Oliver Fforde. Perhaps I can set your mind at rest. Amabel is with me and quite safe. She will explain everything to you, but I promise you that you have no need to worry about her.' He handed the phone back. 'I'll take the dogs for a quick walk—tell Miss Parsons that you will phone again this evening.'

Aunt Thisbe's firm voice begging her to take her time and tell her what had happened collected Amabel's wits for her. She gave a fairly coherent account of what had been happening. 'And Oliver has told me that he has a job waiting for me with an old aunt and has asked me to take it. And I've said I would because I should like to repay his kindness.'

'A sensible decision, child. An opportunity to express your thanks and at the same time give you a chance to decide what you intend to do. I heard Oliver saying that you will phone again this evening. This has changed things, of course. I was thinking of returning for Christmas, so that you would have somewhere to come over the holiday period, but now that there is no need of that and so I shall stay here for another few weeks. But remember, Amabel, if you need me I will return at once. I am very relieved that Oliver has come to your aid. A good man, Amabel, and one to be trusted.'

Amabel put down the phone as Oliver returned. He said briskly, 'I've put the dogs in the car. If you will get your coat, we'll be off.'

He shovelled Oscar into his basket. 'I must be back at the hospital by three o'clock, so I'll drop you off on the way.' He added impatiently, 'I'll explain as we go.'

Since it was obvious to her that he had no intention of saying anything more until it suited him, Amabel did as she was told.

Consumed by curiosity, and a feeling of uncertainty about her future, Amabel had to wait until they were travelling fast down the M1 before the doctor had anything to say other than enquiries as to her comfort.

'We are going to Aldbury in Hertfordshire. It's a small village a few miles from Berkhamsted. My mother is there, arranging for my aunt's return, and she will explain everything to you—time off, salary and so on—and stay overnight to see you settled in. She is very relieved that you have agreed to take the job and you will be very welcomed, both by her and by Mrs Twitchett, the housekeeper, and Nelly.'

Amabel said, 'Your great-aunt might not like me.'

'There is nothing about you to dislike, Amabel.'

A remark which did nothing for her ego. She had never had delusions about herself, but now she felt a nonentity…

The doctor glanced at her as he spoke, at her unassuming profile as she looked steadily ahead. She looked completely unfazed, accepting the way in which he had bulldozed her into an unknown future. He had had no chance to do otherwise; there had been no time, and to have left her there alone in York would have been unthinkable. He said, 'I've rushed you, haven't I? But sometimes one has to take a chance!'

Amabel smiled. 'A lucky chance for me. I'm so grateful, and I'll do my best with your great-aunt. Would you tell me her name?'

'Lady Haleford. Eighty-seven years old, widowed for ten years. No children. Loves her garden, birds, the country and animals. She likes to play cards and cheats. Since her stroke she has become fretful and forgetful and at times rather peevish.' He added, 'No young society, I'm afraid.'

'Well, I have never gone out much, so that doesn't matter.'

When he could spare the time, he reflected, he would take her out. Dinner and dancing, a theatre or concert. He didn't feel sorry for her, Amabel wasn't a girl one could pity, but she deserved some fun and he liked her. He was even, he had to admit, becoming a little fond of her in a brotherly sort of way. He wanted to see her safely embarked on the life she wanted so that she would have the chance to meet people of her own age, marry… He frowned. Time enough for that…

They travelled on in silence, comfortable in each other's company, and after a while he asked, 'Do you want to stop? There's a quiet pub about ten miles ahead; we can let the dogs out there.'

The pub stood back from the road and the car park was almost empty. 'Go on inside,' the doctor told her. 'I'll see to the dogs and make sure Oscar's all right. We can't stay long.'

As long as it's long enough to find the Ladies' thought Amabel, wasting no time.

They had beef sandwiches and coffee, saw to the dogs and got back into the car. Oscar, snoozing in his basket, was hardly disturbed. Life for him had had its ups and downs lately, but now he was snug and safe and Amabel's voice reassured him.

Travelling in a Rolls Royce was very pleasant, reflected Amabel, warm and comfortable and sliding past everything else on the road. And Oliver drove with relaxed skill. She supposed that he was a man who wasn't easily put out.

When he turned off the motorway he said, 'Not long now,' and sure enough, a few miles past Berkhamsted, he took a side turning and then a narrow lane and slowed as they reached Aldbury. It was a charming village, having its origin in Saxon times. There was a village green, a duck pond and a pub close by, and standing a little apart was the church, and beyond the village there was a pleasing vista of parkland and woods. Amabel, staring round her, knew that she would like living here, and hoped that it might be in one of the brick and timber cottages they were passing.

The doctor drove to the far side of the pond and stopped before a house standing on its own. Its front door opened directly onto the pavement— and it was brick and timber, as the others. It had a thatched roof, just as those did, but it was considerably larger and yet looked just as cosy.

He got out and opened Amabel's door. 'Come in and meet my mother again,' he invited. 'I'll come for the dogs and Oscar in a moment.'

The house door had been opened and a short stout woman stood there, smiling. She said comfortably, 'So here you are, Master Oliver, and the young lady…'

'Miss Amabel Parsons. Amabel, this is Mrs Twitchett.'

He bent to kiss her cheek and Amabel offered a hand, aware that as it was being shaken she was being studied closely. She hoped that Mrs Twitchett's smiling nod was a good sign.

The hall was wide with a wood floor, handsomely carpeted, but Amabel had no time to look around her for a door was thrust open and Mrs Fforde came to meet them.

The doctor bent to kiss her. 'No need to introduce you,' he said cheerfully. 'I'll leave you for a moment and see to the dogs and Oscar.'

'Yes, dear. Can you stay?'

'Ten minutes. I've a clinic in a couple of hours.'

'Coffee? It'll be here when you've seen to the dogs. What about the cat?'

'Oscar is a much-travelled beast; he'll present no problems and the garden is walled.'

He went away and Mrs Fforde took Amabel's arm. 'Come and sit down for a moment. Mrs Twitchett will bring the coffee; I'm sure you must need it. I don't suppose Oliver stopped much on the way?'

'Once—we had coffee and sandwiches.'

'But it's quite a drive, even at his speed. Take off your coat and come and sit down.'

'My husband's aunt, Lady Haleford, is old and frail. I expect Oliver has told you that. The stroke has left her in need of a good deal of assistance.

Nothing that requires nursing, you understand, just someone to be there. I hope you won't find it too arduous, for you are young and elderly people can be so trying! She is a charming old lady, though, and despite the fact that she can be forgetful she is otherwise mentally alert. I do hope that Oliver made that clear to you?'

Mrs Fforde looked so anxious that Amabel said at once, 'Yes, he did. I'll do my best to keep Lady Haleford happy, indeed I will.'

'You don't mind a country life? I'm afraid you won't have much freedom.'

'Mrs Fforde, I am so grateful to have a job where Cyril and Oscar can be with me—and I love the country.'

'You will want to let your mother know where you are?' asked Mrs Fforde gently. 'Presently, when you are settled in, phone her. I shall be staying here overnight and will fetch Lady Haleford in the morning.'

The doctor joined them then, and Mrs Twitchett followed him in with a tray of coffee, Tiger and Cyril sidling in behind her.

'Oscar is in the kitchen,' he observed. 'What a sensible animal he is. Mrs Twitchett and Nelly have already fallen for his charms.' He smiled at Amabel and turned to his mother. 'You'll go home tomorrow? I'll try and get down next weekend. You will discuss everything with Amabel before you go? Good.' He drank his coffee and bent to kiss her cheek. 'I'll phone you…'

He laid a hand on Amabel's shoulder. 'I hope you will be happy with my aunt, Amabel. If there are any problems, don't hesitate to tell my mother.'

'All right—but I don't expect any. And thank you, Oliver.'

He was going again out of her life, and this time it was probably for the last time. He had come to her aid, rescued her with speed and a lack of fuss, set her back on her feet once more and was now perfectly justified in forgetting all about her. She offered her hand and her smile lighted up her face. 'Goodbye, Oliver.'

He didn't reply, only patted her shoulder and a moment later he was gone.

'We will go upstairs,' said Mrs Fforde briskly.

'I'll show you your room, and then we will go over the rest of the house so that you will feel quite at home before Lady Haleford arrives. We should be back in time for lunch and I'll leave soon after that. You're sure you can manage?'

'Yes,' said Amabel gravely. 'I'm sure, Mrs Fforde.' It might not be easy at first, but she owed Oliver so much...

They went up the staircase, with its worn oak treads, to the landing above, with several doors on either side and a passage leading to the back of the house.

'I've put you next to my aunt's room,' said Mrs Fforde. 'There's a bathroom between—hers. Yours is on the other side of your room. I hope you won't have to get up in the night, but if you are close by it will make that easier.'

She opened a door and they went in together. It was a large room, with a small balcony overlooking the side of the house, and most comfortably furnished. It was pretty chintz curtains matching the bedspread, thick carpeting and a dear little easy chair beside a small table close to the window. The small dressing table had a stool before it and there was a pink-shaded lamp on the bedside table.

Mrs Fforde led the way across the room and opened a door. 'This is your bathroom—rather small, I'm afraid…'

Amabel thought of the washbasin behind the shop. 'It's perfect,' she said.

'And here's the door to my aunt's bathroom…' They went through it, and on into Lady Haleford's room at the front of the house. It was magnificently furnished, its windows draped in damask, the four-poster bed hung with the same damask, the massive dressing table loaded with silver-backed brushes and mirror, little cut-glass bottles and trinkets.

'Has Lady Haleford always lived here?'

'Yes—at least since her husband died. They lived in the manor house before that, of course, but when her son inherited he moved there with his wife and children and she came here. That was ten years ago. She has often told me that she prefers this house to the manor. For one thing the garden here is beautiful and the rooms aren't too large. And, being in the village, she can still see her friends without having to go too far. Until she had her stroke she drove herself, but of course that won't be possible now. Do you drive?'

'Yes,' said Amabel. 'But I'm not used to driving in large towns.'

'It would be driving Lady Haleford to church and back, and perhaps to call on local friends.'

'I could manage that,' said Amabel.

They went round the house in a leisurely manner. It was, she considered, rather large for one old lady and her two staff, but it was comfortable, rather old-fashioned, and it felt like home. Downstairs, beside the drawing room, there was a dining room, the morning room and a small sitting room—all immaculate. The kind of rooms, reflected Amabel, in which one could sit all day.

The last room they went into was the kitchen, as old-fashioned as the rest of the house. Something smelled delicious as they went in, and Mrs Twitchett turned from the Aga to warn them that dinner would be on the table in half an hour. Nelly was doing something at the table, and sitting before the Aga, for all the world as though they had lived there for ever, were Cyril and Oscar, pleased to see her but making no effort to rouse themselves.

'Happen they're tired out,' said Mrs Twitchett. 'They've eaten their fill and given no trouble.'

Amabel stooped to pat them. 'You really don't mind them being here?'

'Glad to have them. Nelly dotes on them. They'll always be welcome in here.'

Amabel had a sudden urge to burst into tears, a foolishness she supposed, but the relief to have a kind home for her two companions was great. They deserved peace and quiet after the last few months…

She smiled uncertainly at Mrs Twitchett and said thank you, then followed Mrs Fforde out of the kitchen.

Over dinner she was told her duties—not onerous but, as Mrs Fforde pointed out, probably boring and tiring. She was to take her free time when and where she could, and if it wasn't possible to have a day off each week she was to have two half-days. She might have to get up at night occasionally, and, as Mrs Fforde pointed out, the job at times might be demanding. But the wages she suggested were twice as much as Dolores had paid her. Living quietly, thought Amabel, I shall be able to save almost all of them. With a little money behind her she would have a chance to train for a career which would give her future security.

The next morning, buoyed up by high hopes, she waited for Mrs Fforde's return with Lady Haleford. All the same she was nervous.

It was a pity that she couldn't know that the doctor, sitting at his desk in his consulting rooms, had spared a moment to think of her as he studied his next patient's notes. He hoped that she would be happy with his great-aunt; the whole thing had been hurriedly arranged and even now she might be regretting it. But something had had to be done to help her.

He stood up to greet his patient and dismissed her from his thoughts.

Mrs Fforde's elderly Rover stopped in front of the door and Amabel went into the hall, standing discreetly at a distance from Mrs Twitchett and Nelly, waiting at the door. She and Cyril had been out early that morning for a walk through the country lanes; now he stood quietly beside her, and Oscar had perched himself close by, anxious not to be overlooked.

Lady Haleford was small and thin, and walked with a stick and the support of Mrs Fforde's arm, but although she walked slowly and hesitantly there was nothing invalidish about her.

She returned Mrs Twitchett's and Nelly's greetings in a brisk manner and asked at once, 'Well, where's this girl Oliver has found to look after me?'

Mrs Fforde guided her into the drawing room and sat her in a high-backed chair. 'Here, waiting for you.' She said over her shoulder, 'Amabel, come and meet Lady Haleford.'

Amabel put a cautionary finger on Cyril's head and went to stand before the old lady.

'How do you do, Lady Haleford?'

Lady Haleford studied her at some length. She had dark eyes, very bright in her wrinkled face, a small beaky nose and a mouth which, because of her stroke, drooped sideways.

'A plain girl,' she observed to no one in particular. 'But looks are only skin-deep, so they say. Nice eyes and pretty hair, though, and young…' She added peevishly, 'Too young. Old people are boring to the young. You'll be gone within a week. I'm peevish and I forget things and I wake in the night.'

Amabel said gently, 'I shall be happy here, Lady Haleford. I hope you will let me stay and keep you company. This is such a lovely old house, you must be glad to be home again, you will get well again now that you are home.'

Lady Haleford said, 'Pooh,' and then added, 'I suppose I shall have to put up with you.'

'Only for as long as you want to, Lady Haleford,' said Amabel briskly.

'Well, at least you've a tongue in your head,' said the old lady. 'Where's my lunch?'

Her eye fell on Cyril. 'And what's this? The dog Oliver told me about? And there's a cat?'

'Yes. They are both elderly and well-behaved, and I promise you they won't disturb you.'

Lady Haleford said tartly, 'I like animals. Come here, dog.'

Cyril advanced obediently, not much liking to be called dog when he had a perfectly good name. But he stood politely while the old lady looked him over and then patted his head.

Mrs Fforde went home after lunch, leaving Amabel to cope with the rest of the day. Oliver had advised her to let Amabel find her own feet. 'She's quite capable of dealing with any hic-coughs,' he had pointed out, 'and the sooner they get to know each other the better.'

A remark which hadn't prevented him from thinking that perhaps he had made a mistake pitching Amabel into a job she might dislike. She was an independent girl, determined to make a good future for herself; she had only accepted the job with his great-aunt because she had to have a roof over her head and money in her pocket. But he had done his best, he reflected and need waste no more time thinking about her.

But as he had decided not to think any more about Amabel, so Miriam was equally deter-mined to think about him. Dolores had phoned her and told her of his visit. 'I told him that she had left York—I invented an aunt somewhere or other, a friend of her mother's…' She didn't mention that he hadn't believed her. 'He went away and I didn't see him again. Is he back in London? Have you seen him?'

'No, not yet, but I know he's back. I rang his consulting rooms and said I wanted an appoint-ment. He's been back for days. He can't have wasted much time in looking for her. You've been an angel, Dolores, and so clever to fob him off.'

'Anything for a friend, darling. I'll keep my eyes and ears open just in case she's still around.' She giggled. 'Good hunting!'

As far as she was concerned she didn't intend

to do any more about it, although she did once ask idly if anyone had seen Amabel or her visitor when she had her coffee in the patisserie. But the girl behind the counter didn't like Dolores; she had treated Amabel shabbily and she had no need to know that that nice man had gone back one evening and told her that Amabel and her companions were safe with him.

Miriam had phoned Oliver's house several times to be told by Bates that his master was not home.

'He's gone away again?' she'd asked sharply.

'No. No, miss. I assume that he's very busy at the hospital.'

He told the doctor when he returned in the evening. 'Mrs Potter-Stokes, sir, has been ringing up on several occasions. I took it upon myself to say that you were at the hospital. She didn't wish to leave a message.' He lowered his eyes. 'I should have told you sooner, sir, but you have been away from home a good deal.'

'Quite right, Bates. If she should phone again, will you tell her that I'm very busy at the moment? Put it nicely.'

Bates murmured assent, concealing satisfaction; he disliked Mrs Potter-Stokes.

It was entirely by chance that Miriam met a friend of her mother's one morning. A pleasant lady who enjoyed a gossip.

'My dear, I don't seem to have seen you lately. You and Oliver Fforde are usually together…' She frowned. 'He is coming to dinner on Thursday, but someone or other told me that you were away.'

'Away? No, I shall be at home for the next few weeks.' Miriam contrived to look wistful. 'Oliver and I have been trying to meet for days—he's so busy; you would never believe how difficult it is to snatch an hour or two together.'

Her companion, a woman without guile and not expecting it in others, said at once, 'My dear Miriam, you must come to dinner. At least you can sit with each other and have a little time together. I'll get another man to make up the numbers.'

Miriam laid a hand on her arm. 'Oh, how kind of you; if only we can see each other for a while we can arrange to meet.'

Miriam went home well satisfied, so sure of her charm and looks that she was positive that Oliver, seeing her again, would resume their friendship and forget that silly girl.

But she was to be disappointed. He greeted her with his usual friendly smile, listened to her entertaining chatter, and with his usual beautiful manners evaded her questions as to where he had been. It was vexing that despite all her efforts he was still no more than one of her many friends.

At the end of the evening he drove her home, but he didn't accept her invitation to go in for a drink.

'I must be up early,' he told her, and wished her a pleasantly cool goodnight.

Miriam went angrily to her bed. She could find no fault in his manner towards her, but she had lost whatever hold she'd thought she had on him. Which made her all the more determined to do something about it. She had always had everything she wanted since she was a small girl, and now she wanted Oliver.

It was several days later that, an unwilling fourth at one of her mother's bridge parties, she heard someone remark, 'Such a pity he cannot spare the time to join us; he's going away for the weekend…'

The speaker turned to Miriam. 'I expect you knew that already, my dear?'

Miriam stopped herself just in time from trumping her partner's ace.

'Yes, yes, I do. He's very fond of his mother…'

'She lives at such a pleasant place. He's going to see an old aunt as well.' She laughed. 'Not a very exciting weekend for him. You won't be with him, Miriam?' The speaker glanced at her slyly.

'No, I'd already promised to visit an old schoolfriend.'

Miriam thought about that later. There was no reason why Oliver shouldn't visit an old aunt; there was no reason why she should feel uneasy about it. But she did.

She waited for a day or two and then phoned him, keeping her voice deliberately light and understanding. There was rather a good film on; how about them going to see it together at the weekend?

'I'll be away,' he told her.

'Oh, well, another time. Visiting your mother?'

'Yes. It will be nice to get out of London for a couple of days.'

He was as pleasant and friendly as he always had been, but she knew that she was making no headway with him. There was someone else— surely not that girl still?

She gave the matter a good deal of thought, and finally telephoned Mrs Fforde's home; if she was home, she would hang up, say 'wrong number', or make some excuse, but if she was lucky enough to find her out and the housekeeper, a garrulous woman, answered, she might learn something…

She was in luck, and the housekeeper, told that this was an old friend of the doctor's, was quite ready to offer the information that he would be staying for the weekend and leaving early on Sunday to visit Lady Haleford.

'Ah, yes,' said Miriam encouragingly, 'his great-aunt. Such a charming old lady.'

The housekeeper went on, 'Back home after a stroke, madam told me. But they've got someone to live with her—a young lady, but very competent.'

'I must give Lady Haleford a ring. Will you let me have her number?'

It was an easy matter to phone and, under the pretext of getting a wrong number, discover that Lady Haleford lived at Aldbury. It would be wise to wait until after Oliver had been there, but then she would find some reason for calling on the old lady and see for herself what it was about this girl that held Oliver's interest.

Satisfied that she had coped well with what she considered a threat to her future, Miriam relaxed.

Amabel, aware that fate was treating her kindly, set about being as nearly a perfect companion as possible. No easy task, for Lady Haleford was difficult. Not only was she old, she was accustomed to living her life as she wished—an impossibility after her stroke—so that for the first few days nothing was right, although she tolerated Cyril and Oscar, declaring that no one else understood her.

For several days Amabel was to be thoroughly dispirited; she had done nothing right, said nothing right, remained silent when she should have spoken, spoken when she was meant to be silent. It was disheartening, but she liked the old lady and guessed that underneath the peevishness and ill-temper there was a frightened old lady lurking.

There had been no chance to establish any kind of routine. She had had no free time other than brief walks round the garden with Cyril. But Mrs Twitchett and Nelly had done all they could to help her, and she told herself that things would improve.

She had coaxed Lady Haleford one afternoon, swathed in shawls, to sit in the drawing room, and had set up a card table beside her, intent on getting her to play two-handed whist. Her doctor had been that morning, pronounced himself satisfied with her progress and suggested that she might begin to take an interest in life once more.

He was a hearty man, middle-aged and clearly an old friend. He had taken no notice of Lady Haleford's peevishness, told her how lucky she was to have someone so young and cheerful to be with her and had gone away, urging Amabel at the same time to get out into the fresh air.

'Nothing like a good walk when you're young,' he had observed, and Mabel, pining for just that, had agreed with him silently.

Lady Haleford went to sleep over her cards and Amabel sat quietly, waiting for her to rouse herself again. And while she sat, she thought. Her job wasn't easy, she had no freedom and almost no leisure, but on the other hand she had a roof—a comfortable one—over her head, Oscar and Cyril had insinuated themselves into the household and become household pets, and she would be able to save money. Besides, she liked Lady Haleford, she loved the old house and the garden, and she had so much to be thankful for she didn't know where to begin.

With the doctor, she supposed, who had made it all possible. If only she knew where he lived she could write and tell him how grateful she was…

The drawing room door opened soundlessly and he walked in.

Amabel gaped at him, her mouth open. Then she shut it and put a finger to it. 'She's asleep,' she whispered unnecessarily, and felt a warm wave of delight and content at the sight of him.

He dropped a kiss on her cheek, having crossed the room and sat down.

'I've come to tea,' he told her, 'and if my aunt will invite me, I'll stay for supper.'

He sounded matter-of-fact, as though dropping in for tea was something he did often, and he was careful to hide his pleasure at seeing Amabel again. Still plain, but good food was producing some gentle curves and there were no longer shadows under her eyes.

Beautiful eyes, thought the doctor, and smiled, feeling content in her company.

CHAPTER SEVEN

LADY HALEFORD gave a small snort and woke up.

'Oliver—how delightful. You'll stay for tea? Amabel, go and tell Mrs Twitchett. You know Amabel, of course?'

'I saw her as I came in, and yes, I know Amabel. How do you find life now that you are back home, Aunt?'

The old lady said fretfully, 'I get tired and I forget things. But it is good to be home again. Amabel is a good girl and not impatient. Some of the nurses were impatient. You could feel them seething under their calm faces and I can sympathise with them.'

'You sleep well?'

'I suppose so. The nights are long, but Amabel makes tea and we sit and gossip.' She added in an anxious voice, 'I shall get better, Oliver?'

He said gently, 'You will improve slowly, but getting well after illness is sometimes harder than being ill.'

'Yes, it is. How I hate that wheelchair and that horrible thing to help me walk. I won't use it, you know. Amabel gives me an arm...'

The old lady closed her eyes and nodded off for a moment, before adding, 'It was clever of you to find her, Oliver. She's a plain girl, isn't she? Dresses in such dull clothes too, but her voice is pleasant and she's gentle.' She spoke as though Amabel wasn't there, sitting close to her. 'You made a good choice, Oliver.'

The doctor didn't look at Amabel. 'Yes, indeed I did, Aunt.'

Nelly came in with the tea tray then, and he began a casual conversation about his mother and his work and the people they knew, giving Amabel time to get over her discomfort. She was too sensible to be upset by Lady Haleford's remarks, but he guessed that she felt embarrassed...

Tea over, Lady Haleford declared that she would take a nap. 'You'll stay for dinner?' she wanted to know. 'I see you very seldom.' She sounded peevish.

'Yes, I'll stay with pleasure,' he told her. 'While you doze Amabel and I will take the dogs for a quick run.'

'And I shall have a glass of sherry before we dine,' said the old lady defiantly.

'Why not? We'll be back in half an hour or so. Come along, Amabel.'

Amabel got up. 'Is there anything you want before we go, Lady Haleford?' she asked.

'Yes, fetch Oscar to keep me company.'

Oscar, that astute cat, knew on which side his bread was buttered, for he settled down primly on the old lady's lap and went to sleep.

It was cold outside, but there was a bright moon in a starry sky. The doctor took Amabel's arm and walked her briskly through the village, past the church and along a lane out of the village. They each held a dog lead and the beasts trotted beside them, glad of the unexpected walk.

'Well,' said the doctor, 'how do you find your job? Have you settled in? My aunt can be difficult, and now, after her stroke, I expect she is often querulous.'

'Yes, but so should I be. Wouldn't you? And I'm very happy here. It's not hard work, and you know everyone is so kind.'

'But you have to get up during the night?'

'Well, now and then.' She didn't tell him that Lady Haleford woke up during the early hours most nights and demanded company. Fearful of further probing questions, she asked, 'Have you been busy? You haven't needed to go to York again?'

'No, that is a matter happily dealt with. You hear from your mother and Miss Parsons?'

'Yes, Aunt Thisbe is coming home at the end of January, and my mother seems very happy. The market garden is planted and they have plenty of help.' She faltered for a moment. 'Mother said not to go home and see her yet, Mr Graham is still rather—well, I think he'd rather that I didn't visit them...'

'You would like to see your mother?' he asked gently.

'Yes, but if she thinks it is best for me to stay away then I will. Perhaps later…'

'And what do you intend to do later?'

They turned for home and he tucked her hand under his arm.

'Well, I shall be able to save a lot of money. It's all computers these days, isn't it? So I'll take a course in them and get a good job and somewhere to live.' She added anxiously, 'Your aunt does want me to stay for a while?'

'Oh, most certainly. I've talked to her doctor and he thinks that she needs six weeks or two months living as she does at present, and probably longer.'

They had reached the house again.

'You have very little freedom,' he told her.

She said soberly, 'I'm content.'

They had supper early, for Lady Haleford became easily tired, and as soon as the meal was finished the doctor got up to go.

'You'll come again?' demanded his aunt. 'I like visitors, and next time you will tell me about yourself. Haven't you found a girl to marry yet?

You are thirty-four, Oliver. You've enough money and a splendid home and the work you love; now you need a wife.'

He bent to kiss her. 'You shall be the first to know when I find her.' And to Amabel he said, 'No, don't get up. Mrs Twitchett will see me out.' He put a hand on Amabel's shoulder as he passed her chair, and with Tiger at his heels was gone.

His visit had aroused the old lady; she had no wish to go to bed, she said pettishly. And it was a pity that Oliver could visit her so seldom. She observed, 'He is a busy man, and I dare say has many friends. But he needs to settle down. There are plenty of nice girls for him to choose from, and there is that Miriam…' She was rambling a bit. 'The Potter-Stokes widow—been angling for him for an age. If he's not careful she'll have him.' She closed her eyes. 'Not a nice young woman…'

Lady Haleford dozed for a while so Amabel thought about Oliver and the prospect of him marrying. She found the idea depressing, although it was the obvious thing for a man in his position to do. Anyway, it was none of her business.

A week went by, almost unnoticed in the gentle routine of the old house. Lady Haleford improved a little, but not much. Some days her testiness was enough to cast a blight over the entire household, so that Mrs Twitchett burnt the soup and Nelly dropped plates and Amabel had to listen to a diatribe of her many faults. Only Cyril and Oscar weathered the storm and her fierce little rages, sitting by her chair and allowing her peevish words to fly over their heads.

But there were days when she was placid, wanting to talk, play at cards, and walk slowly round the house, carefully hitched up under Amabel's arm.

Her doctor came, assured her that she was making steady progress, warned Amabel to humour her as much as possible and went away again.

Since humouring her meant getting up in the small hours to read to the old lady, or simply to talk until she drowsed off to a light sleep, Amabel had very little time for herself. At least each morning she took Cyril for a walk while

Lady Haleford rested in her bed after breakfast before getting up, and she looked forward to her half-hour's freedom each day, even when it was cold and wet.

On this particular morning it was colder and wetter than it had been for several days, and Amabel, trudging back down the village street with Cyril beside her, looked rather as though she had fallen into a ditch and been pulled out backwards. Her head down against the wind and rain, she didn't see the elegant little sports car outside Lady Haleford's gate until she was beside it.

Even then she would have opened the door and gone inside if the woman in the car hadn't wound down the window and said in an anxious voice, 'Excuse me—if you could spare a moment? Is this Lady Haleford's house? My mother is a friend of hers and asked me to look her up as I was coming this way. But it's too early to call. Could I leave a message with someone?'

She smiled charmingly while at the same time studying Amabel's person. This must be the girl, reflected Miriam. Plain as a pikestaff and looks like a drowned rat. I can't believe that Oliver is in the least bit interested in her. Dolores has been tricking me... She spent a moment thinking of how she would repay her for that, then said aloud, at her most charming, 'Are you her granddaughter or niece? Perhaps you could tell her?'

'I'm Lady Haleford's companion,' said Amabel, and saw how cold the lovely blue eyes were. 'But I'll give her a message if you like. Would you like to come back later, or come and wait indoors? She has been ill and doesn't get up early.'

'I'll call on my way back,' said Miriam. She smiled sweetly. 'I'm sorry you're so wet standing there; I am thoughtless. But perhaps you don't mind the country in winter. I don't like this part of England. I've been in York for a while, and after that this village looks so forlorn.'

'It's very nice here,' said Amabel. 'But York is lovely; I was there recently.'

Her face ringed by strands of wet hair, she broke into a smile she couldn't suppress at the remembrance of the doctor.

Miriam said sharply, 'You have happy memories of it?'

Amabel, lost in a momentary dream, didn't notice the sharpness. 'Yes.'

'Well, I won't keep you.' Miriam smiled and made an effort to sound friendly. 'I'll call again.'

She drove away and Amabel went indoors. She spent the next ten minutes drying herself and Cyril and then went to tidy herself before going to Lady Haleford's room.

The old lady was in a placid mood, not wanting to talk much and apt to doze off from time to time. It wasn't until she was dressed and downstairs in her normal chair by the drawing room fire that she asked, 'Well, what have you been doing with yourself, Amabel?'

Glad of something to talk about, Amabel told her of her morning's encounter. 'And I'm so sorry but she didn't tell me her name, and I forgot to ask, but she said that she'll be back.'

Lady Haleford said worriedly, 'I do have trouble remembering people... What was she like? Dark? Fair? Pretty?'

'Fair and beautiful, very large blue eyes. She was driving a little red car.'

Lady Haleford closed her eyes. 'Well, she'll be back. I don't feel like visitors today, Amabel, so if she does call make my apologies—and ask her name.'

But of course Miriam didn't go back, and after a few days they forgot about her.

Miriam found it just impossible to believe that Oliver could possibly have any interest in such a dull plain girl, but all the same it was a matter which needed to be dealt with. She had begun to take it for granted that he would take her to the theatre, out to dine, to visit picture galleries, and even when he had refused on account of his work she had been so sure of him…

Her vanity prevented her from realising that he had merely been fulfilling social obligations, that he had no real interest in her.

She would have to change her tactics. She stopped phoning him with suggestions that they should go to the theatre or dine out, but she took care to be there at a mutual friend's house if he were to be there, too. Since Christmas was approaching, there were dinner parties and social gatherings enough.

Not that he was always to be found at them. Oliver had many friends, but his social life depended very much on his work so that, much to Miriam's annoyance, she only saw him from time to time, and when they did meet he was his usual friendly self, but that was all. Her pretty face and charm, her lovely clothes and witty talk were wasted on him.

When they had met at a friend's dinner party, and she'd asked casually what he intended to do for Christmas, he'd told her pleasantly that he was far too busy to make plans.

'Well, you mustn't miss our dinner party,' she'd told him. 'Mother will send you an invitation.'

The days passed peacefully enough at Aldbury. Lady Haleford had her ups and downs—indeed it seemed to Amabel that she was slowly losing ground. Although perhaps the dark days of the winter made the old lady loath to leave her bed. Since her doctor came regularly, and assured Amabel that things were taking their course, she spent a good many hours sitting in Lady Haleford's room, reading to her or playing two-handed patience.

All the same she was glad when Mrs Fforde phoned to say that she would be coming to spend a day or two. 'And I'm bringing two of my grandchildren with me—Katie and James. We will stay for a couple of days before I take them to London to do the Christmas shopping. Lady Haleford is very fond of them and it may please her to see them. Will you ask Mrs Twitchett to come to the phone, Amabel? I leave it to you to tell my aunt that we shall be coming.'

It was a piece of news which pleased the old lady mightily. 'Two nice children,' she told Amabel. 'They must be twelve years old—twins, you know. Their mother is Oliver's sister.' She closed her eyes for a moment and presently added, 'He has two sisters; they're both married, younger than he.'

They came two days later; Katie was thin and fair, with big blue eyes and a long plait of pale hair and James was the taller of the two, quiet and serious. Mrs Fforde greeted Amabel briskly.

'Amabel—how nice to see you again. You're rather pale—I dare say that you don't get out enough. Here are Katie and James. Why not take them into the garden for a while and I will visit Lady Haleford? Only put on something warm.' Her eyes lighted on Cyril, standing unexpectedly between the children.

'They are happy, your cat and dog?'

'Yes, very happy.'

'And you, Amabel?'

'I'm happy too, Mrs Fforde.'

Oscar, wishing for a share of the attention, went into the garden too, and, although it was cold, it was a clear day with no wind. They walked along its paths while the children told Amabel at some length about their shopping trip to London.

'We spend Christmas at Granny's,' they explained. 'Our aunt and uncle and cousins will be there, and Uncle Oliver. We have a lovely time and Christmas is always the same each year. Will you go home for Christmas, Amabel?'

'Oh, I expect so,' said Amabel, and before they could ask any more questions added, 'Christmas is such fun, isn't it?'

They stayed for two days, and Amabel was sorry to see them go, but even such a brief visit had tired Lady Haleford, and they quickly slipped back into the placid pattern of their days.

Now that Christmas was near Amabel couldn't help wishing that she might enjoy some of the festivities, so it was a delightful surprise when Lady Haleford, rather more alert than she had been, told her that she wanted her to go to Berkhamstead and do some Christmas shopping. 'Sit down,' she commanded, 'and get a pen and some paper and write down my list.'

The list took several days to complete, for Lady Haleford tended to doze off a good deal, but finally Amabel caught the village bus, her ears ringing with advice and instructions from Mrs Twitchett, the list in her purse and a wad of banknotes tucked away safely.

It was really rather exciting, and shopping for presents was fun even if it was for someone else. It was a long list, for Lady Haleford's family was a large one: books, jigsaw puzzles, games for the younger members, apricots in brandy, a special blend of coffee, Stilton cheese in jars, a case of wine, boxes of candied fruits, and mouth-watering chocolates for the older ones.

Amabel, prowling round the small grocer's shop which seemed to stock every luxury imaginable, had enjoyed every minute of her shopping. She had stopped only briefly for a sandwich and coffee, and now, with an hour to spare before the bus left, she did a little shopping for herself.

High time too, she thought, stocking up on soap and toiletries, stockings and a thick sweater, shampoos and toothpaste. And then presents: patience cards for Lady Haleford, a scarf for Mrs Twitchett, a necklace for Nelly, a new collar for Cyril and a catnip mouse for Oscar. It was hard to find a present for her mother; she chose a blouse, in pink silk, and, since she couldn't ignore him, a book token for her stepfather.

At the very last minute she saw a dress, silvery grey in some soft material—the kind of dress, she told herself, which would be useful for an occasion, and after all it was Christmas… She bought it and, laden with parcels, went back to Aldbury.

The old lady, refreshed by a nap, wanted to see everything. Amabel drank a much needed cup of tea in the kitchen and spent the next hour or so carefully unwrapping parcels and wrapping them up again. Tomorrow, said Lady Haleford, Amabel must go into the village shop and get coloured wrapping paper and labels and write appropriate names on them.

The village shop was a treasure store of Christmas goods. Amabel spent a happy half-hour choosing suitably festive paper and bore it back for the old lady's approval. Later, kneeling on the floor under Lady Haleford's eyes, she was glad of her experience in Dolores's shop, for the gifts were all shapes and sizes. Frequently it was necessary to unwrap something and repack it because Lady Haleford had dozed off and got muddled…

The doctor, coming quietly into the room, unnoticed by a dozing Lady Haleford and, since she had her back to the door, by Amabel, stood in the doorway and watched her. She wasn't quite as tidy as usual, and half obscured by sheets of wrapping paper and reels of satin ribbon. Even from the back, he considered, she looked flustered...

The old lady opened her eyes and saw him and said, 'Oliver, how nice. Amabel, I've changed my mind. Unwrap the Stilton cheese and find a box for it.'

Amabel put down the cheese and looked over her shoulder. Oliver smiled at her and she smiled back, a smile of pure delight because she was so happy to see him again.

Lady Haleford said with a touch of peevishness, 'Amabel—the cheese...'

Amabel picked it up again and clasped it to her bosom, still smiling, and the doctor crossed the room and took it from her.

'Stilton—who is it for, Aunt?' He eyed the growing pile of gaily coloured packages. 'I see you've done your Christmas shopping.'

'You'll stay for lunch?' said Lady Haleford.

'Amabel, go and tell Mrs Twitchett.' When Amabel had gone she said, 'Oliver, will you take Amabel out? A drive, or tea, or something? She has no fun and she never complains.'

'Yes, of course. I came partly to suggest that we had dinner together one evening.'

'Good. Mrs Twitchett told me that the child has bought a new dress. Because it's Christmas, she told her. Perhaps I don't pay her enough…'

'I believe she is saving her money so that she can train for some career or other.'

'She would make a good wife…' The old lady dozed off again.

It was after lunch, when Lady Haleford had been tucked up for her afternoon nap, that the doctor asked Amabel if she would have dinner with him one evening. They were walking the dogs, arm-in-arm, talking easily like two old friends, comfortable with each other, but she stopped to look up at him.

'Oh, that would be lovely. But I can't, you know. It would mean leaving Lady Haleford for a whole evening, and Nelly goes to her mother's

house in the village after dinner—she's got rheu-
matism, her mother, you know—and that means
Mrs Twitchett would be alone…'

'I think that something might be arranged if
you would leave that to me.'

'And then,' continued Amabel, 'I've only one
dress. I bought it the other day, but it's not very
fashionable. I only bought it because it's
Christmas, and I…really, it was a silly thing to do.'

'Since you are going to wear it when we go out
I don't find it in the least silly.' He spoke gently.
'Is it a pretty dress?'

'Pale grey. Very plain. It won't look out of date
for several years.'

'It sounds just the thing for an evening out.
I'll come for you next Saturday evening—half
past seven.'

They walked back then, and presently he went
away, giving her a casual nod. 'Saturday,' he
reminded her, and bent to kiss her cheek. Such
a quick kiss that she wasn't sure if she had
imagined it.

She supposed that she wasn't in the least surprised to find that Lady Haleford had no objection to her going out with the doctor. Indeed, she seemed to find nothing out of the ordinary in it, and when Amabel enquired anxiously about Nelly going to her mother, she was told that an old friend of Mrs Twitchett's would be spending the evening with her.

'Go and enjoy yourself,' said that lady. 'Eat a good dinner and dance a bit.'

So when Saturday came Amabel got into the grey dress, took pains with her face and her hair and went downstairs to where the doctor was waiting. Lady Haleford had refused to go to bed early; Mrs Twitchett would help her, she had told Amabel, but Amabel was to look in on her when she got home later. 'In case I am still awake and need something.'

Amabel, the grey dress concealed by her coat, greeted the doctor gravely, pronounced herself ready, bade the old lady goodnight, bade Oscar and Cyril to be good and got into the car beside Oliver.

It was a cold clear night with a bright moon.

There would be a heavy frost by morning, but now everything was silvery in the moonlight.

'We're not going far,' said the doctor. 'There's rather a nice country hotel—we can dance if we feel like it.'

He began to talk about this and that, and Amabel, who had been feeling rather shy, lost her shyness and began to enjoy herself. She couldn't think why she should have felt suddenly awkward with him; after all, he was a friend—an old friend by now...

He had chosen the hotel carefully and it was just right. The grey dress, unassuming and simple but having style, was absorbed into the quiet luxury of the restaurant.

The place was festive, without being overpoweringly so, and the food was delicious. Amabel ate prawns and Caesar salad, grilled sole and straw potatoes and, since it was almost Christmas, mouthwatering mince pies with chantilly cream. But not all at once.

The place was full and people were dancing. When the doctor suggested that she might like to dance she got up at once. Only as they reached the dance floor she hesitated. 'It's ages since I danced,' she told him.

He smiled down at her. 'Then it's high time you did now,' he told her.

She was very light on her feet, and she hadn't forgotten how to dance. Oliver looked down onto her neat head of hair and wondered how long it would be before she discovered that she was in love with him. He was prepared to wait, but he hoped that it wouldn't be too long…!

The good food, the champagne and dancing had transformed a rather plain girl in a grey dress into someone quite different. When at length it was time to leave, Amabel, very pink in the cheeks and bright of the eye, her tongue loosened by the champagne, told him that she had never had such a lovely evening in her life before.

'York seems like a bad dream,' she told him, 'and supposing you hadn't happened to see me, what would I have done? You're my guardian angel, Oliver.'

The doctor, who had no wish to be her guardian

angel but something much more interesting, said cheerfully, 'Oh, you would have fallen on your feet, Amabel, you're a sensible girl.'

And all the things she suddenly wanted to say to him shrivelled on her tongue.

'I've had too much champagne,' she told him, and talked about the pleasures of the evening until they were back at Lady Haleford's house.

He went in with her, to switch on lights and make sure all was well, but he didn't stay. She went to the door with him and thanked him once again for her lovely evening.

'I'll remember it,' she told him.

He put his arms round her then, and kissed her hard, but before she could say anything he had gone, closing the door quietly behind him.

She stood for a long time thinking about that kiss, but presently she took off her shoes and crept upstairs to her room. There, was no sound from Lady Haleford's bedroom and all was still when she peeped through the door; she undressed and prepared for bed, and was just getting into bed when she heard the gentle tinkling of the old lady's bell. So she got out of bed again and went quietly to see what was the matter.

Lady Haleford was now wide awake, and wanted an account of the evening.

'Sit down and tell me about it,' she commanded. 'Where did you go and what did you eat?'

So Amabel stifled a yawn and curled up in a chair by the bed to recount the events of the evening. Not the kiss, of course.

When she had finished Lady Haleford said smugly, 'So you had a good time. It was my suggestion, you know—that Oliver should take you out for the evening. He's so kind, you know—always willing to do a good turn. Such a busy man, too. I'm sure he could ill spare the time.' She gave a satisfied sigh. 'Now go to bed Amabel. We have to see to the rest of those Christmas presents tomorrow.'

So Amabel turned the pillow, offered a drink, turned the night light low and went back to her room. In her room she got into bed and closed her eyes, but she didn't go to sleep.

Her lovely evening had been a mockery, a

charitable action undertaken from a sense of duty by someone whom she had thought was her friend. He was still her friend, she reminded herself, but his friendship was mixed with pity.

Not to be borne, decided Amabel, and at last fell asleep as the tears dried on her cheeks.

Lady Haleford had a good deal more to say about the evening out in the morning; Amabel had to repeat everything she had already told her and listen to the old lady's satisfied comments while she tied up the rest of the parcels.

'I told Oliver that you had bought a dress...'

Amabel cringed. Bad enough that he had consented to take her out; he probably thought that she had bought it in the hope that he might invite her.

She said quickly, 'We shall need some more paper. I'll go and buy some...'

In the shop, surrounded by the village ladies doing their weekly shopping, she felt better. She was being silly, she told herself. What did it matter what reason Oliver had had for asking her out for the evening? It had been a lovely surprise and she had enjoyed herself, and what had she expected, anyway?

She went back and tied up the rest of the presents, and recounted, once again, the previous evening's events, for the old lady protested that she had been told nothing.

'Oh, you spent five minutes with me when you came in last night, but I want to know what you talked about. You're a nice girl, Amabel, but I can't think of you as an amusing companion. Men do like to be amused, but I dare say Oliver found you pleasant enough; he can take his pick of pretty women in London.'

All of which did nothing to improve Amabel's spirits.

Not being given to self-pity, she told herself to remember that Lady Haleford was old and had been ill and didn't mean half of what she said. As for her evening out, well, that was a pleasant memory and nothing more. If she should see the doctor again she would take care to let him see that, while they were still friends, she neither expected nor wanted to be more than that.

I'll be a little cool, reflected Amabel, and in a few weeks I expect I'll be gone from here. Being a sensible girl, she fell to planning her future...

This was a waste of time, actually, for Oliver was planning it for her; she would be with his aunt for several weeks yet—time enough to think of a way in which they might see each other frequently and let her discover for herself that he was in love with her and wanted to marry her. He had friends enough; there must be one amongst them who needed a companion or something of that sort, where Cyril and Oscar would be acceptable. And where he would be able to see her as frequently as possible...

The simplest thing would be for her to stay at his house. Impossible—but he lingered over the delightful idea...

He wasn't the only one thinking about Amabel's future. Miriam, determined to marry Oliver, saw Amabel as a real threat to her plans.

She was careful to be casually friendly when she and Oliver met occasionally, and she took care not to ask him any but the vaguest questions about his days. She had tried once or twice to get information from Bates, but he professed ignorance of his employer's comings and goings. He told her stolidly that the doctor was either at his consulting room or at the hospital, and if she phoned and wanted to speak to him at the weekend Bates informed her that he was out with the dog.

Oliver, immersed in his work and thoughts of Amabel, dismissed Miriam's various invitations and suggestions that they might spend an evening together with good-mannered friendliness; he didn't believe seriously that Miriam wanted anything more than his company from time to time; she had men-friends enough.

He underestimated her, though. Miriam drove herself to Aldbury, parked the car away from the centre of the village and found her way to the church. The village shop would have been ideal ground from which to glean information, but there was the risk of meeting Amabel. Besides, people in the village might talk.

The church was old and beautiful, but she

didn't waste time on it. Someone—the vicar, she supposed—was coming down the aisle towards her, wanting to know if he could help her…

He was a nice elderly man, willing to talk to this charming lady who was so interested in the village. 'Oh, yes,' he told her, 'there are several old families living in the village, their history going back for many years.'

'And those lovely cottages with thatched roofs—one of them seems a good deal larger than the rest?'

'Ah, yes, that would be Lady Haleford's house. A very old family. She has been ill and is very elderly. She was in hospital for some time, but now I'm glad to say she is at home again. There is a very charming young woman who is her companion. We see her seldom, for she has little spare time, although Lady Haleford's nephew comes to visit his aunt and I have seen the pair of them walking the dogs. He was here recently, so I'm told, and took her out for the evening…! How I do ramble on, but living in a small village we tend to be interested in each other's doings. You are touring this part of the country?'

'Yes, this is a good time of year to drive around the countryside. I shall work my way west to the Cotswolds,' said Miriam, untruthfully. 'It's been delightful talking to you, Vicar, and now I must get back to my car and drive on.'

She shook hands and walked quickly back to her car, watched by several ladies in the village shop, whose sharp eyes took in every inch of her appearance.

She drove away quickly and presently pulled up on the grass verge the better to think. At first she was too angry to put two thoughts together. This was no passing attraction on Oliver's part; he had been seeing this girl for some time now and his interest was deep enough to cause him to seek her out. Miriam seethed quietly. She didn't love Oliver; she liked him enough to marry him and she wanted the things the marriage would bring to her: a handsome husband, money, a lovely home and the social standing his name and profession would give her.

She thumped the driving wheel in rage. Something would have to be done, but what?

CHAPTER EIGHT

QUIET though the routine of Lady Haleford's household was, Christmas, so near now, was not to be ignored. Cards were delivered, gifts arrived, visitors called to spend ten minutes with the old lady, and Amabel trotted round the house arranging and rearranging the variety of pot plants they brought with them.

It was all mildly exciting, but tiring for the invalid, so that Amabel needed to use all her tact and patience, coaxing callers to leave after the briefest of visits, and even then Lady Haleford exhibited a mixture of lethargy and testiness which prompted her to get the doctor to call.

He was a rather solemn man who had looked after the old lady for years, and he now gave it as his opinion that, Christmas or no Christmas, his patient must revert to total peace and quiet.

'The occasional visitor,' he allowed, and Amabel was to use her discretion in turning away more than that.

Amabel said, 'Lady Haleford likes to know who calls. She gets upset if someone she wishes to see is asked not to visit her. I've tried that once or twice and she gets rather uptight.'

Dr Carr looked at her thoughtfully. 'Yes, well, I must leave that to your discretion, Miss Parsons. Probably to go against her wishes would do more harm than good. She sleeps well?'

'No,' said Amabel. 'Although she dozes a lot during the day.'

'But at night—she is restless? Worried…?'

'No. Just awake. She likes to talk, and some-times I read to her.'

He looked at her as though he hadn't really seen her before.

'You get sufficient recreation, Miss Parsons?'

Amabel said that, yes, thank you, she did. Because if she didn't he might decide that she wasn't capable enough for the job and arrange for a nurse. Her insides trembled at the thought.

So Amabel met visitors as they were ushered into the hall and, unless they were very close old friends or remote members of Lady Haleford's family, persuaded them that she wasn't well enough to have a visitor, then offered notepaper and a pen in case they wanted to write a little note and plied them with coffee and one of Mrs Twitchett's mince pies.

Hard work, but it left both parties satisfied.

Though it was quite quiet in the house, the village at its doorstep was full of life. There was a lighted Christmas tree, the village shop was a blaze of fairy lights, and carol singers—ranging from small children roaring out the first line of 'Good King Wenceslas' to the harmonious church choir—were a nightly event. And Mrs Twitchett, while making sure that Lady Haleford was served the dainty little meals she picked at, dished up festive food suitable to the season for the other three of them.

Amabel counted her blessings and tried not to think about Oliver.

* * *

Dr Fforde was going to Glastonbury to spend Christmas with his mother and the rest of his family. Two days which he could ill spare. He had satisfied himself that his patients were making progress, presented the theatre staff with sherry, his ward sister and his receptionist and the nurse at the consulting rooms with similar bottles, made sure that Bates and his wife would enjoy a good Christmas, loaded the car boot with suitable presents and, accompanied by Tiger, was ready to leave home.

He was looking forward to the long drive, and, more than that, he was looking forward to seeing Amabel, for he intended to call on his aunt on his way.

He had been working hard for the last week or so, and on top of that there had been the obligatory social events. Many of them he had enjoyed, but not all of them. He had found the dinner party given by Miriam's parents particularly tedious, but he had had no good reason to refuse the invitation—although he had been relieved to find that Miriam seemed no longer to look upon him as her future. She had been as amusing and attractive as always, but she had made no demands on his time, merely saying with apparent sincerity that he must be glad to get away from his work for a few days.

It was beginning to snow when he left, very early on the morning of Christmas Eve. Tiger, sitting very upright beside him, watched the heavy traffic. It took some time to get away from London but the doctor remained patient, thinking about Amabel, knowing that he would be seeing her in an hour or so.

The village looked charming as he drove through it and there was a small lighted Christmas tree in the cottage's drawing room window. He got out of the car, opened the door for Tiger, and saw Amabel and Cyril at the far end of the village street. Tiger, scenting friends, was already on his way to meet them. Oliver saw Amabel stop, and for a moment he thought she was going to turn round and hurry away. But she bent to greet Tiger and came towards him. He met her halfway.

There was snow powdering her woolly cap and

her coat, and her face was rosy with cold. He thought she looked beautiful, though he was puzzled by her prim greeting.

He said cheerfully, 'Hello. I'm on my way to spend Christmas with the family. How is my aunt?'

'A bit tired,' she told him seriously. 'There have been a great many visitors, although she has seen only a handful of them.'

They were walking back towards the house. 'I expect you'd like to see her? She'll be finishing her breakfast.' Since he didn't speak, the silence got rather long. 'I expect you've been busy?' Annabel finally ventured.

'Yes, I'll go back on Boxing Day.' They had reached the front door when he said, 'What's the matter, Amabel?'

She said, too quickly, 'Nothing. Everything is fine.' And as she opened the door added, 'Would you mind going up to Lady Haleford? I'll dry the dogs and tidy myself.'

Mrs Twitchett came bustling into the hall then, and Amabel slipped away. Oliver wouldn't stay long and she could keep out of his way...

The dogs made themselves comfortable on either side of Oscar in front of the Aga, and when Nelly came in to say that Mr Oliver would have a cup of coffee before he went away Amabel slipped upstairs. Lady Haleford would be ready to start the slow business of dressing.

'Go away,' said the old lady as Amabel went into her room. 'Go and have coffee with Oliver. I'll dress later.' When Amabel looked reluctant, she added, 'Well, run along. Surely you want to wish him a happy Christmas?'

So Amabel went downstairs again, as slowly as possible, and into the drawing room. The dogs and Oscar had gone there with the coffee, sitting before the fire, and the doctor was sitting in one of the big wing chairs.

He got up as she went in, drew a balloon-backed chair closer to his own and invited her to pour their coffee.

'And now tell me what is wrong,' he said kindly. 'For there is something, isn't there? Surely we are friends enough for you to tell me? Something I have done, Amabel?'

She took a gulp of coffee. 'Well, yes, but it's silly of me to mind. So if it's all the same to you I'd rather not talk about it.'

He resisted the urge to scoop her out of her chair and wrap her in his arms. 'It isn't all the same to me…'

She put down her cup and saucer. 'Well, you didn't have to take me out to dinner just because Lady Haleford said that you should—I wouldn't have gone if I'd known…' She choked with sudden temper. 'Like giving a biscuit to a dog…'

Oliver bit back a laugh, not of amusement but of tenderness and relief. If that was all…

But she hadn't finished. 'And I didn't buy a dress because I hoped you would take me out.' She looked at him then. 'You are my friend, Oliver, and that is how I think of you—a friend.'

He said gently, 'I came to take you out for the evening, Amabel. Anything my aunt said didn't influence me in any way. And as for your new dress, that was something I hadn't considered. It was a pretty dress, but you look nice whatever you are wearing.' He would have liked to have said a great deal more, but it was obviously not the right moment. When she didn't speak, he said, 'Still friends, Amabel?'

'Yes—oh, yes, Oliver. I'm sorry I've been so silly.'

'We'll have another evening out after Christmas. I think that you will be here for some time yet.'

'I'm very happy here. Everyone in the village is so friendly, and really I have nothing to do.'

'You have very little time to yourself. Do you get the chance to go out—meet people—young people?'

'Well, no, but I don't mind.'

He got up to go presently. It was still snowing and he had some way to drive still. She went with him to the door, and Tiger, reluctant to leave Cyril and Oscar, pushed between them. Amabel bent to stroke him.

'Go carefully,' she said, 'and I hope that you and your family have a lovely Christmas.'

He stood looking down at her. 'Next year will be different!' He fished a small packet from a pocket. 'Happy Christmas, Amabel,' he said, and kissed her.

He didn't wait to hear her surprised thanks. She stood watching the car until it was out of sight, her mouth slightly open in surprise, clutching the little gaily wrapped box.

The delightful thought that he might come again on his way back to London sent a pleasant glow through her person.

She waited until Christmas morning before she opened the box, sitting up in bed early in the darkness. The box contained a brooch, a true lover's knot, in gold and turquoise—a dainty thing, but one she could wear with her very ordinary clothes.

She got up dressed in the grey dress and pinned the brooch onto it before getting into her coat and slipping out of the house to go to church.

It was dark and cold, and although the snow had stopped it lay thick on the ground. The church was cold too, but it smelled of evergreens and flowers, and the Christmas tree shone with its twinkling lights. There weren't many people at the service, for almost everyone would be at Matins during the morning, but as they left the church there was a pleasant flurry of cheerful talk and good wishes.

Amabel made sure that Lady Haleford was still asleep, had a quick breakfast with Mrs Twitchett and Nelly and took Cyril for his walk. The weather didn't suit his elderly bones and the walk was brief. She settled him next to Oscar by the Aga and went to bid Lady Haleford good morning.

The old lady wasn't in a festive mood. She had no wish to get out of her bed, no wish to eat her breakfast, and she said that she was too tired to look at the gifts Amabel assured her were waiting for her downstairs.

'You can read to me,' she said peevishly.

So Amabel sat down and read. *Little Women* was a soothing book, and very old-fashioned. She found the chapter describing Christmas and the simple pleasures of the four girls and their mother was a sharp contrast to the comfortable life Lady Haleford had always lived.

Presently Lady Haleford said, 'What a horrid old woman I am…'

'You're one of the nicest people I know,' said Amabel, and, quite forgetting that she was a paid companion, she got up and hugged the old lady.

So Christmas was Christmas after all, with presents being opened, and turkey and Christmas pudding and mince pies, suitably interposed between refreshing naps, and Amabel, having tucked Lady Haleford into her bed, went early to bed herself. There was nothing else to do, but that didn't matter. Oliver would be returning to London the next day, and perhaps he would come and see them again…

But he didn't. It was snowing again, and he couldn't risk a hold-up on the way back to London.

The weather stayed wintry until New Year's Day, when Amabel woke to a bright winter's sun and blue sky. It was still snowy underfoot, and as she sloshed through it with a reluctant Cyril she wondered what the New Year would bring…

As for the doctor, he hardly noticed which day of the week it was, for the New Year had brought with it the usual surge of bad chests, tired hearts and the beginnings of a flu epidemic. He left home early and came home late, and ate whatever food Bates put before him. He was tired, and often frustrated, but it was his life and his work, and presently, when things had settled down again, he would go to Amabel...

Miriam waited for a few days before phoning Oliver. He had just got home after a long day and he was tired, but that was something she hadn't considered. There was a new play, she told him, would he get tickets? 'And we could have supper afterwards. I want to hear all about Christmas...'

He didn't tell her that he was working all day and every day, and sometimes into the night as well. He said mildly, 'I'm very busy, Miriam, I can't spare the time. There is a flu epidemic...'

'Oh, is there? I didn't know. There must be plenty of junior doctors...'

'Not enough.'

She said with a flash of temper, 'Then I'll get someone who will enjoy my company.'

The doctor, reading the first of a pile of reports

on his desk, said absent-mindedly, 'Yes, do. I hope you will have a pleasant evening.'

He put the phone down and then picked it up again. He wanted to hear Amabel's voice. He put it down again. Phone conversations were unsatisfactory, for either one said too much or not enough. He would go and see her just as soon as he could spare the time. He ignored the pile of work before him and sat back and thought about Amabel, in her grey dress, wearing, he hoped, the true lover's knot.

Miriam had put down the phone and sat down to think. If Oliver was busy then he wouldn't have time to go to Aldbury. It was a chance for her to go, talk to the girl, convince her that he had no interest in her, that his future and hers were as far apart as two poles. It would be helpful if she could get Amabel away from this aunt of his, but she could see no way of doing that. She would have to convince Amabel that she had become an embarrassment to him…

There was no knowing when Oliver would go to Aldbury again, and Miriam waited with impatience for the snow to clear away. On a cold bright day, armed with a bouquet of flowers purporting to come from her mother, she set out.

The church clock was striking eleven as she stopped before Lady Haleford's cottage. Nelly answered the door, listened politely to Miriam's tale of her mother's friendship with Lady Haleford and bade her come in and wait. Lady Haleford was still in her room, but she would fetch Miss Parsons down. She left Miriam in the drawing room and went away, and presently Amabel came in.

Miriam said at once, 'Oh, hello—we've met before, haven't we? I came at the wrong time. Am I more fortunate today? Mother asked me to let Lady Haleford have these flowers…'

'Lady Haleford will be coming down in a few minutes,' said Amabel, and wondered why she didn't like this visitor.

She was being friendly enough, almost gushing, and Lady Haleford, when Nelly had mentioned Miriam's name, had said, 'That young woman—very pushy. And I haven't met her mother for years.' She had added, 'But I'll come down.'

Which she did, some ten minutes later, leaving Amabel to make polite conversation that Miriam made no effort to sustain.

But with the old lady she was at her most charming, giving her the flowers with a mythical message from her mother, asking about her health with apparent concern.

The old lady, normally a lady of perfect manners, broke into her chatter. 'I am going to take a nap. Amabel, fetch your coat and take Mrs Potter-Stokes to look round the village or the church if she chooses. Mrs Twitchett will give you coffee in half an hour's time. I will say goodbye now; please thank your mother for the flowers.'

She sat back in her chair and closed her eyes, leaving Amabel to usher an affronted Miriam out of the room. In the hall Amabel said, 'Lady Haleford has been very ill and she tires easily. Would you like to see round the church?'

Miriam said no, in a snappy voice, and then, mindful of why she had come, added with a smile, 'But perhaps we could walk a little way out of the village? The country looks very pretty.'

Amabel got into her coat, tied a scarf over her head and, with Cyril on his lead, led the way past the church and into the narrow lane beyond. Being a friendly girl, with nice manners, she made small talk about the village and the people who lived in it, aware that her companion hadn't really wanted to go walking—she was wearing the wrong shoes for a start.

Annoyed though Miriam was, she saw that this was her chance—if only there was a suitable opening. She stepped into a puddle and splashed her shoe and her tights and the hem of her long coat, and saw the opening...

'Oh, dear. Just look at that. I'm afraid I'm not a country girl. It's a good thing that I live in London and always shall. I'm getting married soon, and Oliver lives and works there too...'

'Oliver?' asked Amabel in a careful voice.

'A nice name, isn't it? He's a medical man, always frightfully busy, although we manage to get quite a lot of time together. He has a lovely house; I shall love living there.'

She turned to smile at Amabel. 'He's such a dear—very kind and considerate. All his patients dote on him. And he's always ready to help any lame dog over a stile. There's some poor girl he's saved from a most miserable life—gone out of his way to find her a job. I hope she's grateful. She has no idea where he lives, of course. I mean, she isn't the kind of person one would want to become too familiar with, and it wouldn't do for her to get silly ideas into her head, would it?'

Amabel said quickly, 'I shouldn't think that would be very likely, but I'm sure she must be grateful.'

Miriam tucked a hand under Amabel's arm. 'Oh, I dare say—and if she appeals to him again for any reason I'll talk to her. I won't have him badgered; heaven knows how many he's helped without telling me. Once we're married, of course, things will be different.'

She gave Amabel a smiling nod, noting with

satisfaction that the girl looked pale. 'Could we go back? I'm longing for a cup of coffee...'

Over coffee she had a great deal to say about the approaching wedding. 'Of course, Oliver and I have so many friends, and he's well known in the medical profession. I shall wear white, of course...' Miriam allowed her imagination full rein.

Amabel ordered more coffee, agreed that four bridesmaids would be very suitable, and longed for her unwelcome visitor to go. Which, presently, she did.

Lady Haleford, half dozing in her room, opened her eyes long enough to ask if the caller had gone and nodded off again, for which Amabel was thankful. She had no wish to repeat their conversation—besides, Oliver's private life was none of her business. She hadn't liked Miriam, but it had never entered her head that the woman was lying. It all made sense; Oliver had never talked about his home or his work or his friends. And why should he? Mrs Twitchett had remarked on several occasions that he had given unobtrusive help to people. 'He's a very private person,' she had told Amabel. 'Lord knows what goes on in that clever head of his.'

There was no hope of going to see Amabel for the moment; the flu epidemic had swollen to a disquieting level. The doctor treated his patients with seeming tirelessness, sleeping when he could, sustained by Mrs Bates's excellent food and Bates's dignified support. But Amabel was always at the back of his mind, and from time to time he allowed himself to think about her, living her quiet life and, he hoped, sometimes thinking about him.

Of Miriam he saw nothing; she had prudently gone to stay with friends in the country, where there was less danger of getting the flu. She phoned him, leaving nicely calculated messages to let him see that she was concerned about him, content to bide her time, pleased with herself that she had sewn the seeds of doubt in Amabel's mind. Amabel was the kind of silly little fool, she reflected, who would believe every word of what she had said. Head over heels in love with him, thought Miriam, and doesn't even know it.

But here she was wrong; Amabel, left unhappy and worried, thought about Oliver a good deal. In fact he was never out of her thoughts. She *had* believed Miriam when she had told her that she and Oliver were to marry. If Lady Haleford hadn't been particularly testy for the next few days she might have mentioned it to her, but it wasn't until two o'clock one morning, when the old lady was sitting up in her bed wide awake and feeling chatty, that she began to talk about Oliver.

'Time he settled down. I only hope he doesn't marry that Potter-Stokes woman. Can't stand her—but there's no denying that she's got looks and plenty of ambition. He'd be knighted in no time if she married him, for she knows all the right people. But he'd have a fashionable practice and turn into an embittered man. He needs to be loved…'

Amabel, curled up in a chair by the bed, wrapped in her sensible dressing gown, her hair neatly plaited, murmured soothingly, anxious that the old lady should settle down. Now was certainly not the time to tell her about Miriam's news.

Lady Haleford dozed off and Amabel was left with her thoughts. They were sad, for she agreed wholeheartedly with the old lady that Miriam would not do for Oliver. He does need someone to love him, reflected Amabel, and surprised herself by adding *me*.

Once over her surprise at the thought, she allowed herself to daydream a little. She had no idea where Oliver lived—somewhere in London—and she knew almost nothing about his work, but she would love him, and care for him, and look after his house, and there would be children…

'I fancy a drop of hot milk,' said Lady Haleford. 'And you'd better go to bed, Amabel. You looked washed out…'

Which effectively put an end to daydreams, although it didn't stop her chaotic thoughts. Waiting for the milk to heat, she decided that she had been in love with Oliver for a long time, accepting him into her life as naturally as drawing breath. But there was nothing to be done about it; Miriam had made it plain that he wouldn't welcome the prospect of seeing her again.

If he did come to see his aunt, thought Amabel, pouring the milk carefully into Lady Haleford's special mug, then she, Amabel, would keep out of his way, be coolly pleasant, let him see that she quite understood.

These elevating thoughts lasted until she was back in her own bed, where she could cry her eyes out in peace and quiet.

The thoughts stood her in good stead, for Oliver came two days later. It being a Sunday, and Lady Haleford being in a good mood, Amabel had been told that she might go to Matins, and it was on leaving the church that she saw the car outside the cottage. She stopped in the porch, trying to think of a means of escape. If she went back into the church she could go out through the side door and up the lane and stay away for as long as possible. He probably wasn't staying long…

She felt a large heavy arm on her shoulders and turned her head.

'Didn't expect me, did you?' asked the doctor cheerfully. 'I've come to lunch.'

Amabel found her voice and willed her heart to stop thumping. She said, 'Lady Haleford will be pleased to see you.'

He gave her a quick, all-seeing look. Something wasn't quite right…

'I've had orders to take you for a brisk walk before lunch. Up the lane by the church?'

Being with him, she discovered, was the height of happiness. Her high-minded intentions could surely be delayed until he had gone again? While he was there, they didn't make sense. As long as she remembered that they were friends and nothing more.

She said, 'Where's Tiger?'

'Being spoilt in the kitchen. Wait here. I'll fetch him and Cyril.'

He was gone before she could utter, and soon back again with the dogs, tucking an arm in hers and walking her briskly past the church and up the lane. The last time she had walked along it, she reflected, Miriam had been with her.

Very conscious of the arm, she asked, 'Have you been busy?'

'Very busy. There's not been much flu here?'

'Only one or two cases.' She sought for something to talk about. 'Have you seen Lady Haleford yet? She's better—at least I think so. Once the spring is here, perhaps I could drive her out sometimes—just for an hour—and she's looking forward to going into the garden.'

'I spent a few minutes with her. Yes, she is making progress, but it's a long business. I should think you will be here for some weeks. Do you want to leave, Amabel?'

'No, no, of course not. Unless Lady Haleford would like me to go?'

'That is most unlikely. Have you thought about the future?'

'Yes, quite a lot. I—I know what I want to do. I'll go and see Aunt Thisbe and then I'll enrol at one of those places where I can train to use a computer. There's a good one at Manchester; I saw it advertised in Lady Haleford's paper.' She added, to make it sound more convincing, 'I've saved my money, so I can find somewhere to live.'

The doctor, quite rightly, took this to be a spur-of-the-moment idea, but he didn't say so.

'Very sensible. You don't wish to go home?'

'Yes. I'd like to see Mother, but she wrote to me just after Christmas and said that my stepfather still wasn't keen for me to pay a visit.'

'She could come here…'

'I don't think he would like that. I did suggest it.' she added, 'Mother is very happy. I wouldn't want to disturb that.'

They had been walking briskly and had passed the last of the cottages in the lane. The doctor came to a halt and turned her round to face him.

'Amabel, there is a great deal I wish to say to you…'

'No,' she said fiercely. 'Not now—not ever. I quite understand, but I don't want to know. Oh, can't you see that? We're friends, and I hope we always will be, but when I leave here it's most unlikely that we shall meet again.'

He said slowly, 'What makes you think that we shall never meet again?'

'It wouldn't do,' said Amabel. 'And now please don't let's talk about it any more.'

He nodded, his blue eyes suddenly cold. 'Very well.' He turned her round. 'We had better go back, or Mrs Twitchett will be worried about a spoilt lunch.'

He began to talk about the dogs and the weather, and was she interested in paintings? He had been to see a rather interesting exhibition of an early Victorian artist…

His gentle flow of talk lasted until they reached the cottage again and she could escape on the pretext of seeing if the old lady needed anything before lunch. The fresh air had given her face a pleasing colour, but it still looked plain in her mirror. She flung powder onto her nose, dragged a comb through her hair and went downstairs.

Lady Haleford, delighted to have Oliver's company, asked endless questions. She knew many of the doctor's friends and demanded news of them.

'And what about you, Oliver? I know you're a busy man, but surely you must have some kind of social life?'

'Not a great deal—I've been too busy.'

'That Potter-Stokes woman called—brought flowers from her mother. Heaven knows why; I hardly know her. She tired me out in ten minutes. I sent her out for a walk with Amabel…'

'Miriam came here?' asked Oliver slowly, and looked at Amabel, sitting at the other side of the table.

She speared a morsel of chicken onto her fork and glanced at him quickly. 'She's very beautiful, isn't she? We had a pleasant walk and a cup of coffee—she couldn't stay long; she was on her way to visit someone. She thought the village was delightful. She was driving one of those little sports cars…' She stopped talking, aware that she was babbling.

She put the chicken in her mouth and chewed it. It tasted like ashes.

'Miriam is very beautiful,' agreed the doctor, staring at her, and then said to his aunt, 'I'm sure you must enjoy visitors from time to time, Aunt, but don't tire yourself.'

'I don't. Besides, Amabel may look like a mouse, but she can be a dragon in my defence. Bless the girl! I don't know what I would do without her.' After a moment she added, 'But of course she will go soon.'

'Not until you want me to,' said Amabel. 'And by then you will have become so much better that you won't need anyone.' She smiled across the table at the old lady. 'Mrs Twitchett has made your favourite pudding. Now, there is someone you would never wish to be without!'

'She has been with me for years. Oliver, your Mrs Bates is a splendid cook, is she not? And Bates? He still runs the place for you?'

'My right hand,' said the doctor. 'And as soon as you are well enough I shall drive you up to town and you can sample some of Mrs Bates's cooking.'

Lady Haleford needed her after-lunch nap.

'Stay for tea?' she begged him. 'Keep Amabel company. I'm sure you'll have plenty to talk about…'

'I'm afraid that I must get back.' He glanced at his watch. 'I'll say goodbye now.'

When Amabel came downstairs again he had gone.

Which was only to be expected, Amabel told herself, but she would have liked to have said goodbye. To have explained…

But how did one explain that, since one had fallen in love with someone already engaged to someone else, meeting again would be pointless. And she had lost a friend…

Later that day Lady Haleford, much refreshed by her nap, observed, 'A pity Oliver had to return so soon.' She darted a sharp glance at Amabel. 'You get on well together?'

'Yes,' said Amabel, and tried to think of something to add but couldn't.

'He's a good man.'

'Yes,' said Amabel again. 'Shall I unpick that knitting for you, Lady Haleford?'

The old lady gave her a thoughtful look. 'Yes, Amabel, and then we will have a game of cards. That will distract our thoughts.'

Amabel, surveying her future during a wakeful
night, wondered what she should do, but as
events turned out she had no need to concern
herself with that.

It was several days after Oliver's visit that she
had a phone call. She had just come in with Cyril,
after his early-morning walk, and, since Nelly
and Mrs Twitchett were both in the kitchen, she
answered it from the phone in the hall.

'Is that you, Amabel?' Her stepfather's voice
was agitated. 'Listen, you must come home at
once. Your mother's ill—she's been in hospital
and they've sent her home and there's no one to
look after her.'

'What was wrong? Why didn't you let me
know that she was ill?'

'It was only pneumonia. I thought they'd keep
her there until she was back to normal. But here
she is, in bed most of the day, and I've enough
to do without nursing her as well.'

'Haven't you any help?'

'Oh, there's a woman who comes in to clean
and cook. Don't tell me to hire a nurse; it's your

duty to come home and care for your mother. And I don't want any excuses. You're her daughter, remember.'

'I'll come as soon as I can,' said Amabel, and took Cyril to the kitchen.

Mrs Twitchett looked at her pale face. 'Something wrong? Best tell us.'

It was a great relief to tell someone. Mrs Twitchett and Nelly heard her out.

'Have to go, won't you love?' Nelly's eye fell on Cyril and Oscar, side by side in front of the Aga. 'Will you take them with you?'

'Oh, Nelly, I can't. He wanted to kill them both; that's why I left home.' Amabel sniffed back tears. 'I'll have to take them to a kennel and a cattery.'

'No need,' Mrs Twitchett said comfortably. 'They'll stay here until you know what's what. Lady Haleford loves them both, and Nelly will see to Cyril's walks. Now, just you go and tell my lady what it's all about.'

Lady Haleford, sitting up in bed, sipping her early-morning tea and wide awake for once, said

immediately, 'Of course you must go home immediately. Don't worry about Cyril and Oscar. Get
your mother well again and then come back to us.
Will she want you to stay at home for good?'

Amabel shook her head. 'No, I don't think so.
You see, my stepfather doesn't like me.'

'Then go and pack, and arrange your journey.'

CHAPTER NINE

THE doctor had driven himself back to London, deep in thought. It was obvious that Miriam had said something to Amabel which had upset her and caused her to retire into her shell of coolness. But she hadn't sounded cool in the lane. The only way to discover the reason for this was to go and see Miriam. She had probably said something as a joke and Amabel had misunderstood her...

He had gone to see her the very next evening and found her entertaining friends. As she had come to meet him he had said, 'I want to talk to you, Miriam.'

She, looking into his bland face and cold eyes, said at once, 'Oh, impossible, Oliver—we're just about to go out for the evening.'

'You can join your friends later. It is time we had a talk, Miriam, and what better time than now?'

She pouted. 'Oh, very well.' Then she smiled enchantingly. 'I was beginning to think that you had forgotten me.'

Presently, when everyone had gone, she sat down on a sofa and patted the cushion beside her. 'My dear, this is nice—just the two of us.'

The doctor sat down in a chair opposite her.

'Miriam, I have never been your dear. We have been out together, seen each other frequently at friends' houses, visited the theatre, but I must have made it plain to you that that was the extent of our friendship.' He asked abruptly, 'What did you say to Amabel?'

Miriam's beautiful face didn't look beautiful any more. 'So that's it—you've fallen in love with that dull girl! I guessed it weeks ago, when Dolores saw you in York. Her and her silly pets. Well, anyway, I've cooked your goose. I told her you were going to marry me, that you had helped her out of kindness and the sooner she disappeared the better...'

She stopped, because Oliver's expressionless face frightened her, and then when he got to his feet said, 'Oliver, don't go. She's no wife for you; you need someone like me, who knows everyone worth knowing, entertains all the right people, dresses well.'

Oliver walked to the door. 'I need a wife who loves me and whom I love.' And he went away.

It was a pity, he reflected that his next few days were so crammed with patients, clinics and theatre lists that it was impossible for him to go and see Amabel. It was a temptation to phone her, but he knew that would be unsatisfactory. Besides, he wanted to see her face while they talked.

He drove back home and went to his study and started on the case notes piled on his desk, dismissing Amabel firmly from his thoughts.

Lady Haleford had summoned Mrs Twitchett to her bedroom and demanded to know how Amabel was to go home. 'I don't know where the girl lives. Didn't someone tell me that she came from York?'

'And so she did, my lady; she's got an aunt there. Left home when her mother brought in a stepfather who don't like her. Somewhere near Castle Cary—she'll need to get the train to the nearest station and get a taxi or a bus, if there is one.'

Mrs Twitchett hesitated. 'And, my lady, could we keep Oscar and Cyril here while she's away? Seeing that her stepfather won't have them? Going to put them down, he was, so she left home.'

'The poor child. Arrange for William down at the village garage to drive her home. I've already told her that of course the animals must stay.'

So Amabel was driven away in the village taxi, which was just as well, for the journey home otherwise would have been long and tedious and she had had no time to plan it.

It was late afternoon when William drew up with a flourish at her home.

There were lights shining from several windows, and she could see a large greenhouse at the side of the house. As they got out of the car she glimpsed another beyond it, where the orchard had been.

The front door opened under her touch and they went into the hall as she saw her stepfather come from the kitchen.

'And about time too,' he said roughly. 'Your mother's in the sitting room, waiting to be helped to bed.'

'This is William, who brought me here by taxi,' said Amabel. 'He's going back to Aldbury, but he would like a cup of tea first.'

'I've no time to make tea…'

Amabel turned to William. 'If you'll come with me to the kitchen, I'll make it. I'll just see Mother first.'

Her mother looked up as she went into the sitting room.

'There you are, Amabel. Lovely to see you again, dear, and have you here to look after me.' She lifted her face for Amabel's kiss. 'Keith is quite prepared to let bygones be bygones and let you live here…'

'Mother, I must give the taxi driver a cup of tea. I'll be back presently and we can have a talk.'

There was no sign of her stepfather. William,

waiting patiently in the kitchen, said, 'Not much of a welcome home, miss.'

Amabel warmed the teapot. 'Well, it all happened rather suddenly. Do you want a sandwich?'

William went very soon, feeling all the better for the tea and sandwiches, and the tip he had accepted reluctantly, and Amabel went back to the sitting room.

'Tell me what has been wrong with you, Mother. Do you stay up all day? The doctor visits you?'

'Pneumonia, love, and I went to hospital because Keith couldn't possibly manage on his own.'

'Have you no help?'

'Oh, yes, of course. Mrs Twist has been coming each day, to see to the house and do some of the cooking, and the hospital said a nurse would come each day once I was back home. She came for a day or two, but she and Keith had an argument and he told them that you would be looking after me. Not that I need much attention. In fact he's told Mrs Twist that she need not come any more, now that you are back home.'

'My stepfather told me that there was no one to look after you, that he had no help…'

Her mother said lightly, 'Oh, well, dear, you know what men are—and it does seem absurd for him to pay for a nurse and Mrs Twist when we have you…'

'Mother, I don't think you understand. I've got a job. I came because I thought there was no one to help you. I'll stay until you are better, but you must get Mrs Twist back and have a nurse on call if it's necessary. I'd like to go back to Aldbury as soon as possible. You see, dear, Keith doesn't like me—but you're happy with him, aren't you?'

'Yes, Amabel, I am, and I can't think why you can't get on, the pair of you. But now you are here the least you can do is make me comfortable. I'm still rather an invalid, having breakfast in bed and then a quiet day here by the fire. My appetite isn't good, but you were always a good cook. Keith likes his breakfast early, so you'll have all day to see to the house.'

She added complacently, 'Keith is doing very

well already, and now he won't need to pay Mrs Twist and that nurse he can plough the money back. You'll want to unpack your things, dear. Your old room, of course. I'm not sure if the bed is made up, but you know where everything is. And when you come down we'll decide what we'll have for supper.'

Of course the bed wasn't made up; the room was chilly and unwelcoming and Amabel sat down on the bed to get her thoughts sorted out. She wouldn't stay longer than it took to get Mrs Twist back, see the doctor and arrange for a nurse to visit, whatever her stepfather said. She loved her mother, but she was aware that she wasn't really welcome, that she was just being used as a convenience by her stepfather.

She made the bed, unpacked, and went back downstairs to the kitchen. There was plenty of food in the fridge. At least she wouldn't need to go to the shops for a few days…

Her mother fancied an omelette. 'But that won't do for Keith. There's a gammon steak, and you might do some potatoes and leeks. You won't have time to make a pudding, but there's plenty of cheese and biscuits…'

'Have you been cooking, Mother?'

Her mother said fretfully, 'Well, Keith can't cook, and Mrs Twist wasn't here. Now you're home I don't need to do anything.'

The next morning Amabel went to the village to the doctor's surgery. He was a nice man, but elderly and overworked.

'You're mother is almost fit again,' he assured Amabel. 'There is no reason why she shouldn't do a little housework, as long as she rests during the day. She needs some tests done, of course, and pills, and a check-up by the practice nurse. It is a pity that her husband refuses to let her visit; he told me that you would be coming home to live and that you would see to your mother.'

'Has Mother been very ill?'

'No, no. Pneumonia is a nasty thing, but if it's dealt with promptly anyone as fit as your mother makes a quick recovery.'

'I understood from what my stepfather told me on the phone that Mother was very ill and he was without help.' She sighed. 'I came as quickly as I could, but I have a job…'

'Well, I shouldn't worry too much about that. I imagine that a few days of help from you will enable your mother to lead her usual life again. She has help, I believe?'

'My stepfather gave Mrs Twist notice…'

'Oh, dear, then you must get her back. Some-one local?'

'Yes.'

'Well, it shouldn't be too difficult to persuade Mr Graham to change his mind. Once she is re-instated, you won't need to stay.'

Something which she pointed out to her step-father later that day. 'And do please understand that I must go back to my job at the end of week. The doctor told me that Mother should be well by then. You will have to get Mrs Twist to come every day.'

'You unnatural girl.' Keith Graham's face was red with bad temper. 'It's your duty to stay here…'

'You didn't want me to stay before,' Amabel pointed out quietly. 'I'll stay for a week, so that you have time to make arrangements to find someone to help Mother.' She nodded her neat head at him. 'There was no need for me to come home. I love Mother, but you know as well as I do that you hate having me here. I can't think why you decided to ask me to come.'

'Why should I pay for a woman to come and do the housework when I've a stepdaughter I can get for nothing?'

Amabel got to her feet. If there had been something suitable to throw at him she would have thrown it, but since there wasn't she merely said, 'I shall go back at the end of the week.'

But there were several days to live through first, and although her mother consented to be more active there was a great deal to do—the cooking, fires to clean and light, coal to fetch from the shed, beds to make and the house to tidy. Her stepfather didn't lift a finger, only coming in for his meals, and when he wasn't out and about he was sitting by the fire, reading his paper.

Amabel said nothing, for eventually there was only one more day to go...

She was up early on the last morning, her bag packed, and she went down to cook the breakfast Keith demanded. He came into the kitchen as she dished up his bacon and eggs.

'Your mother's ill,' he told her. 'Not had a wink of sleep—nor me neither. You'd better go and see to her.'

'At what time is Mrs Twist coming?'

'She isn't. Haven't had time to do anything about her…'

Amabel went upstairs and found her mother in bed.

'I'm not well, Amabel. I feel awful. My chest hurts and I've got a headache. You can't leave me.'

She moaned as Amabel sat her gently against her pillows.

'I'll bring you a cup of tea, Mother, and phone the doctor.'

She went downstairs to phone and leave a message at the surgery. Her stepfather said angrily. 'No need for him. All she needs is a few days in bed. You can stay on a bit.'

'I'll stay until you get Mrs Twist back. Today, if possible.'

Her mother would eat no breakfast, so Amabel helped her to the bathroom, made the bed and tidied the room and then went back downstairs to cancel the taxi which was to have fetched her in an hour's time. She had no choice but to stay until the doctor had been and Mrs Twist was reinstated.

There was nothing much wrong with her mother, the doctor told her when he came. She was complaining about her chest, but he could find nothing wrong there, and her headache was probably due to the sleepless nights she said she was having.

He said slowly, 'She has worked herself up because you are going away. I think it would be best if you could arrange to stay for another day or two. Has Mr Graham got Mrs Twist to come in?'

'No. He told me that he had had no time. I thought I might go and see her myself. You don't think that Mother is going to be ill again?'

'As far as I can see she has recovered completely from the pneumonia, but, as I say, she has worked herself up into a state—afraid of being ill again. So if you could stay…'

'Of course I'll stay until Mother feels better.' She smiled at him. 'Thank you for coming, Doctor.'

He gave her a fatherly pat. He thought she looked a bit under the weather herself he must remember to call in again in a day or two.

Amabel unpacked her bag, assured her mother that she would stay until Mrs Twist could come, and went to see that lady…

Mrs Twist was a comfortable body with a cheerful face. She listened to Amabel in silence and then said, 'Well, I'm sorry to disoblige you, but I've got my old mum coming today for a week. Once she's gone home again I'll go each day, same as before. Staying long, are you?'

'I meant to go back to my job this morning, but Mother asked me to stay until you could arrange to come back.' She couldn't help adding, 'You will come, won't you?'

'Course I will, love. And a week goes by quick enough. Nice having your ma to chat to.'

Amabel said, yes, it was, and thought how nice

that would have been. Only there was precious little time to chat, and when she did sit down for an hour to talk it was her mother who did the talking: about how good Keith was to her, the new clothes she had bought, the holiday they intended to take before the spring brought all the extra work in the greenhouses, how happy she was… But she asked no questions of Amabel.

She said, 'I expect you've got a good job, darling. You were always an independent girl. You must tell me about it one day…I was telling you about our holiday…'

It was strange how the days seemed endless, despite the fact that she had little leisure. She had written a note to Lady Haleford, saying that she would return as soon as she could arrange help for her mother. Since her mother seemed quite well again, it was now just a question of waiting for Mrs Twist's mother to go home. Her mother, however, was disinclined to do much.

'There's no need for me to do anything,' she had said, half laughing, 'while you're here.'

'Mrs Twist does everything when she comes?'

'Oh, yes. Although I do the cooking. But you're such a good cook, love, and it gives you something to do.'

One more day, thought Amabel. She had missed Cyril and Oscar. She had missed Oliver too, but she tried not to think of him—and how could she miss someone she hardly ever saw?

Amabel had been gone for almost two weeks before the doctor felt free to take time off and go to Aldbury. His aunt greeted him with pleasure. 'But you've come to see Amabel? Well, she's not here. The child had to go home; her mother was ill. She expected to be gone for a week. Indeed, she wrote and told me she would be coming back. And then I had another letter saying that she would have to stay another week. Can't think why she didn't telephone.' She added, 'Mrs Twitchett phoned and a man answered her. Very abrupt, she said, told her that Amabel wasn't available.'

It was already late afternoon, and the doctor had a list early on the following morning, a clinic in the afternoon and private patients to see. To get into his car and go to Amabel was something he wanted to do very much, but that wasn't possible; it wouldn't be possible for two days.

He thought about phoning her, but it might make matters worse and in any case there was a great deal he could do. He went back home, sat down at his desk and picked up the phone; he could find out what was happening...

Mrs Graham's doctor was helpful. There was no reason, he said over the phone, why Amabel should stay at home. She had told him very little, but he sensed that her mother's illness had been used to get her to return there. 'If there is anything I can do?' he offered.

'No, no, thanks. I wanted to be sure that her mother really needs her.'

'There's no reason why she shouldn't walk out of the house, but there may be circumstances which prevent her doing that.'

The doctor picked up the phone and heard Miss Parsons' firm voice at the other end.

'I hoped that you might be back...' He talked

at some length and finally put the phone down and went in search of Bates. After that, all he had to do was to possess his soul in patience until he could go to Amabel.

He set off early in the morning two days later, with Tiger beside him and Bates to see him on his way.

Life was going to be quite interesting, Bates thought as he went in search of his wife.

Once free of London and the suburbs, Oliver drove fast. He hoped that he had thought of everything. A lot was going to happen during the next few hours, and nothing must go wrong.

It was raining when he reached the house, and now that the apple orchard had gone the house looked bare and lonely and the greenhouses looked alien. He drove round the side of the house, got out with Tiger, opened the kitchen door and went in.

Amabel was standing at the sink, peeling potatoes. She was wearing an apron several sizes too large for her and her hair hung in a plait over one shoulder. She looked pale and tired and utterly forlorn.

This was no time for explanations; the doctor strode to the sink, removed the potato and the knife from her hands and folded his arms around her. He didn't speak, he didn't kiss her, just held her close. He was holding her when Mr Graham came in.

'Who are you?' he demanded.

Oliver gave Amabel a gentle push. 'Go and get your coat and pack your things.' Something in his voice made her disentangle herself from his embrace and look up at his quiet face. He smiled down at her. 'Run along, darling.'

She went upstairs and all she could think of then was that he had called her darling. She should have taken him into the sitting room, where her mother was… Instead she got her case from the wardrobe and began to pack it, and, that done, picked up her coat and went downstairs.

The doctor had watched her go and then turned to Mr Graham, who began in a blustering voice, 'I don't know why you're here, whoever you are—'

'I'll tell you,' said Oliver gently. 'And when I've finished perhaps you will take me to Amabel's mother.'

She looked up in surprise as they went into the sitting room.

'He's come for Amabel,' said Mr Graham, looking daggers at Oliver. 'I don't know what things are coming to when your daughter's snatched away and you so poorly, my dear.'

'Your doctor tells me that you are fully recovered, Mrs Graham, and I understand that you have adequate help in the house…'

'I'm very upset—' began Mrs Graham. Glancing at the quiet man standing there, she decided that a show of tears wouldn't help. 'After all, a daughter should take care of her mother…'

'And do the housework and the cooking?' From the look of her Amabel has been doing that, and much more besides.

'She ought to be grateful,' growled Mr Graham, 'having a home to come to.'

'Where she is expected to do the chores, cook and clean and shop?' asked Oliver coolly. 'Mr Graham, you make me tired—and extremely angry.'

'Who is going to see to things when she's gone?'

'I'm sure there is adequate help to be had in the village.' He turned away as Amabel came into the room. 'Everything is satisfactorily arranged,' he told her smoothly. 'If you will say goodbye, we will go.'

Amabel supposed that presently she would come to her senses and ask a few sensible questions, even ask for an explanation of the unexpected events taking place around her, but all she said was, 'Yes, Oliver,' in a meek voice, and went to kiss her mother and bid her stepfather a frosty goodbye.

She said tartly, 'There's a lot I could say to you, but I won't,' and she walked out of the room with Oliver. Tiger was in the kitchen, and somehow the sight of him brought her to her senses.

'Oliver—' she began.

'We'll talk as we go,' he told her comfortably, and popped her into the car, settled Tiger in the back seat and got in beside her. Presently he said in a matter-of-fact voice, 'We shall be home in time for supper. We'll stop at Aldbury and get Oscar and Cyril.'

'But where are we going?'

'Home.'

'I haven't got a home,' said Amabel wildly.

'Yes, you have.' He rested a hand on her knee for a moment. 'Darling, *our* home.'

And after that he said nothing for quite some time, which left Amabel all the time in the world to think. Chaotic thoughts which were interrupted by him saying in a matter-of-fact voice, 'Shall we stop for a meal?' and, so saying, stopping before a small pub, well back from the road, with a lane on one side of it.

It was dim and cosy inside, with a handful of people at the bar, and they had their sandwiches and coffee against a background of cheerful talk, not speaking much themselves.

When they had finished the doctor said, 'Shall we walk a little way up the lane with Tiger?'

They walked arm in arm and Amabel tried to think of something to say—then decided that there was no need; it was as though they had everything that mattered.

But not quite all, it seemed, for presently, when

they stopped to look at the view over a gate, Oliver turned her round to face him.

'I love you. You must know that, my dear. I've loved you since I first saw you, although I didn't know it at once. And then you seemed so young, and anxious to make a life for yourself; I'm so much older than you…'

Amabel said fiercely, 'Rubbish. You're just the right age. I don't quite understand what has happened, but that doesn't matter…' She looked up into his face. 'You have always been there, and I can't imagine a world without you…'

He kissed her then, and the wintry little lane was no longer a lane but heaven.

In a little while they got back into the car, and Amabel, with a little gentle prompting, told Oliver of her two weeks with her mother.

'How did you know I was there?' she wanted to know, and when he had told her she said, 'Oliver, Miriam Potter-Stokes said that you were going to marry her. I know now that wasn't true, but why did she say that?' She paused. 'Did you think that you would before you met me?'

'No, my darling. I took her out once or twice, and we met often at friends' houses. But it never entered my head to want to marry her. I think that she looked upon me, as she would look upon any other man in my position, as a possible source of a comfortable life.'

'That's all right, then,' said Amabel.

She looked so radiantly happy that he said, 'My dearest, if you continue to look like that I shall have to stop and kiss you.'

An unfulfilled wish since they were on a motorway.

There was no doubt about the warmth of their welcome at Lady Haleford's cottage. They were met in the hall by Mrs Twitchett, Nelly, Oscar and Cyril, and swept into the drawing room, where Lady Haleford was sitting.

She said at once, 'Amabel, I am so happy to see you again, although I understand from Oliver that this visit is a brief one. Still, we shall see more of each other, I have no doubt. I shall miss you and Oscar and Cyril. Oliver shall bring you here whenever he has the time, but of course first of all he must take you to see his mother. You'll marry soon?'

Amabel went pink and Oliver answered for her. 'Just as soon as it can be arranged, Aunt.'

'Good. I shall come to the wedding, and so will Mrs Twitchett and Nelly. Now we will have tea…'

An hour later, once more in the car, Amabel said, 'You haven't asked me…'

He glanced at her briefly, smiling. 'Oh, but I will. Once we are alone and quiet. I've waited a long time, dear love, but I'm not going to propose to you driving along a motorway.'

'I don't know where you live…'

'In a quiet street of Regency houses. There's a garden with a high wall, just right for Oscar and Cyril, and Bates and his wife look after me and Tiger, and now they will look after you three as well.'

'Oh—is it a big house?'

'No, no, just a nice size for a man and his wife and children to live in comfortably.'

Which gave Amabel plenty to think about,

staring out of the window into the dark evening through rose-coloured spectacles, soothed by Oliver's quiet voice from time to time and the gentle fidgets of the three animals on the back seat.

She hadn't been sure of what to expect, and when she got out of the car the terrace of houses looked elegant and dignified, with handsome front doors and steps leading to their basements. But Oliver gave her time to do no more than glimpse at them. Light streamed from an open door and someone stood waiting by it.

'We're home,' said Oliver, and took her arm and tucked it under his.

She had been feeling anxious about Bates, but there was no need; he beamed at her like a kindly uncle, and Mrs Bates behind him shook her hand, her smile as wide as her husband's.

'You will wish to go straight to the drawing room, sir,' said Bates, and opened a door with a flourish.

As they went in, Aunt Thisbe came to meet them.

'Didn't expect to see me, did you, Amabel?' she asked briskly. 'But Oliver is a stickler for the conventions, and quite right too. You will have to bear with me until you are married.'

She offered a cheek to be kissed, and then again for Oliver.

'You two will want to talk, but just for a moment there is something I need to do…' he murmured.

Aunt Thisbe made for the door. 'I'll see about those animals of yours,' she said, and closed the door firmly behind her.

The doctor unbuttoned Amabel's coat, tossed it on a chair and took her in his arms. 'This is a proposal—but first, this…' he bent his head and kissed her, taking his time about it.

'Will you marry me, Amabel?' he asked her.

'Will you always kiss me like that?' she asked him.

'Always and for ever, dearest.'

'Then I'll marry you,' said Amabel, 'because I like being kissed like that. Besides, I love you.'

There was only one answer to that…